LYING WITH DEMONS

BOOK TWO OF THE CASTILLIAN BLOOD SERIES

KILLIAN WOLF

ISBN - 978-1-951140-05-2

Editor: Claerie Kavanaugh - claeriekavanaugh.com/need-an-editor
Copyeditor: saltandsagebooks.com
Cover design: miblart.com
Formatter: Grim House Publishing LLC - grimhousepub.com/plans-pricing

For mom, who filled my imagination with the love for Halloween and the supernatural.

CONTENTS

My life changed when I was brought back from the dead. They say you never appreciate what you have until it's gone. For some, it's their partner, for others, it's a parent or sibling. But for me, it was being wiped from their memory. A year ago, I would sit at the corner of my sick father's bed while my sister tended to him. But my sister couldn't remember I was her brother nor that the man she was hired to care for was her father. And my father couldn't remember that my sister was his daughter, or that I was dead.

One thing I learned during that time was that everything comes to pass. Nothing is permanent, and those you love will love you unconditionally, even if they don't remember you. In the end, it is the heart that remembers when your mind is fogged, or in my father and sister's case, a spell that had been cast upon them.

Today, I watch as others go through similar pains. I wait in hospital rooms, sometimes a bedroom, sometimes even the street, while someone meets their untimely death. I watch as loved ones cry over them until it's time for me to guide them away from the life they've always known. It sounds morbid, I know. And it is. But don't get me wrong. For the first time in my life, I feel like I am making a difference.

I follow close behind Ambrose as he opens the next portal.

Ambrose leads the way into a quiet nursing home. "After this one, we can go visit your sister."

I nod, shooting him a sideways look. "I could use the break." I haven't always been fond of the idea of Ambrose dating my sister, with him being a reaper and all. What kind of life can they have together? Reapers aren't allowed to have relations with humans, and a life of secrecy isn't what I want for Addison. But, as time passes, I've come to realize that Addison can handle herself. My eyes land on tubes coming out of a man's nose, connected to a machine. "So, who do we have here?"

"Clany Rogers, eighty-seven years old. Remember to keep an eye on the scythe meter. His time is up in a few seconds."

I lower my eyes to my scythe's inner blade where there is a thin meter that measures the amount of time left for each appointment. Each scythe has a unique insignia for its reaper. No one knows the height of a scythe's magick, but its primary purpose is, of course, the reaping of souls.

My scythe gives a soft blue glow. It is time.

"Little by little, you'll get the hang of when it's time. You'll just feel it, instead of waiting for your scythe to glow. You're up."

I move forward as the man's spirit sits up on the bed.

"Who are you?" the man says.

"I am here to tell you there is no more pain. And to guide you out of this plane."

The old man looks down at his body as the machine next to him flatlines. A nurse who had been nearby walks in silently. "I am ready. My wife is waiting for me."

"That's right, Clany. This is not the end."

Ambrose takes his scythe and opens a portal. The three of us step through, and I lead the man to the left, where a young woman with shoulder-length hair, wearing a red dress, waits for him. The old man's wrinkles fade away as he transforms into a younger version of himself. He looks back at me and smiles. I nod back and wave him off.

"Does that feeling ever get old?"

"What feeling?" Ambrose asks.

"The feeling of having accomplished something beautiful, in reuniting loved ones, and in easing the pain of someone's death."

Ambrose puts his hand on my shoulder. "I think you feel it differently than I do because you were once human, and I have always been a reaper. But no, it doesn't get old. Shall we?"

I tuck my scythe inside of my jacket. "Ready when you are."

I take a step back to give Ambrose some room to open the portal into my father's house. Normally, we would just step into the next appointment, but since we're taking a leisurely break, it requires a bit of rerouting. We stand in the cold, dark bridge, used when we guide a recently deceased to their pathway.

Ambrose takes out his scythe and holds it out in front of him.

I raise an eyebrow "Bit theatrical, don't you think?"

"Shhh." Ambrose waves at me to come closer.

"What's wrong?"

"My scythe isn't opening the portal."

A dark fog descends on the bridge. I take my scythe out. "Mine doesn't open portals yet. What do we do?"

"Something is wrong," Ambrose says, chafing his chin and turning his scythe around in his hand, inspecting the blade. "I was given complete clearance to work without Deacon months ago. It can't be because of me."

"Well, what else has the power to shut down a reaper's scythe?"

"To my knowledge, nothing." He lowers his scythe and peers through the blackness.

"Ambrose?"

"What?"

"Look at your scythe."

His scythe flutters red. "I'm not doing that," Ambrose says. "I've never seen it turn red before." It flutters a few more times before the glow strengthens, burning his hands, making him drop his scythe to the bridge. My mouth gapes as a loud echo from the blade hitting the ground sounds through the abyss. A portal opens in front of us.

"Do we go in?" I ask.

"Watch out!" Ambrose yells as two figures grab me from behind.

Still in shock, I bend over, flipping one over my head. The second figure clings onto me, stretches its lips and reveals sharp fangs. I let out a hoarse scream as it bites down on my arm. I fling my arm upward and body slam the creature on the bridge. That's when I get a good look at the fucker. Tall, pointy ears stick up from its head like a bat with glowing red eyes and a long snout. I kick it hard in its stomach as more of these Anubis look-alikes jump down on the bridge, landing on their hind legs. Sharp fangs overlap their lips, protruding along the length of their muzzles.

We're surrounded. I hold a firm grip over the hilt of my scythe, swinging at as many as I can before a hot sensation emanates from the scythe. I flick my gaze down as the handle scorches my palm; the blade too changed from a blue glow to red. The burning handle sticks to me at first and I struggle to open my hand. I drop it and start swinging as hard as I can with my fists. Although I know there's no way in hell I can take them all at once.

I take a glance over at Ambrose, who has his fair share of these mongrels clinging on to him. One of them attacks him from his front while two others hold back his arms. I fall to my knees as one of them kicks my legs from behind, allowing three others to pin me down to the bridge. I jerk my body, trying to get free as one of them stands on my back. Footsteps echo on the far end of the bridge. I arch my head upward, wrinkling my forehead for a better look.

A tall, hooded demon with twisted horns sticking out steps up from the direction of the portal. He reaches down and collects the two fallen scythes.

"Who are you?" Ambrose says. No answer comes. Only heavy breathing from the creatures holding us both down. I watch in horror as the hooded figure uses Ambrose's scythe to cut him slowly from his throat down to his stomach, forming an Enochian sigil that glows when he finishes. Ambrose's face becomes rigid as his eyes gloss over. I wince at his cries as the demon then pushes him through the portal.

I jerk and kick as the Anubis demons continue to swarm over me as the hooded figure takes slow strides in my direction. Black gloves slide out from his cloak as he lifts one of our scythes up to my neck, the blade a sharp glowing red now. Even though he's close enough for me to see him, his hood does a good job at hiding his features, all but a pair of glowing red eyes and black horns with twisting gold veins.

He smiles, showing perfect white teeth. "Hmm, you're different."

"What do you want? Who are you?" my voice croaks before I too am pushed through the portal.

UNEXPECTED VISITOR

ADDISON

*B*lue. The color of the hospital patrician screens I work in every day, and also the color of my patient's new home. Jimmy Hale has no idea where he is or who I am, although I like to hope he recognizes the sound of my voice. I often speak to him while I work, telling him how he's doing and if it's feeding time, just in case it makes a difference. A difference between swimming in a sea of consciousness, not ever wanting to leave, and following the voice back to this plane of existence.

After waking up from a memory curse four months ago, I was also brought back to this plane of existence—in a way. I had no idea who I really was, nor that my patient at the time was suffering under the clutches of a memory demon. He wasn't considered comatose but slept all day and night and would awaken only to eat—and only if I prompted him to. He had no idea who I was, nor that I was his daughter. And I didn't know either. Nor that my boss was my dead brother trying to keep our family together, desperate for a way to break the curse.

It's no surprise I find comfort in caring for comatose

patients now. The steady beeping of his heart rate monitor serenades the atmosphere as I speak to him in a soft and slow cadence. If I'm to reach his subconscious, this is a trick from spellwork my dad has taught me over the years to penetrate the mind and reach the unconscious.

"Alright, Mr. Hale, here we are. Are you ready for your lunch?" Unwrapping a new feeding tool, I quickly make my way to his bedside and take his arm.

"Addison?"

"Oh, Seth, good, you're here. Help me move him after this, will you? Don't want our patient developing body sores." And Seth can put his toned biceps he unintentionally flaunts from his tight fitted scrubs to good use.

"Of course, I just came in to help."

"Thanks."

"And to ask you out to lunch."

I resist the urge to roll my eyes as I finish inserting the central venous catheter into Mr. Hale's large vein. Seth's been a great friend since I started my job at Seashore Memorial Hospital a few months ago. And as much as we do have a lot in common as far as our humor, same taste in movies, and the more obvious one being the need to help others, I need to put a bit of distance between us because he'll ask me out any chance he gets. I know, not exactly great friend material. He usually does respect the fact that I have a boyfriend, but Ambrose isn't always available to hang out with my friends and when he does have time, I like to keep him to myself. What can I say? I'm selfish.

This past week though, Ambrose has been busier than usual showing my brother the ropes on reaping. Which I am beyond grateful for because that means my brother is a reaper-in-training and I can see him. It's almost as if he never died. Ambrose got me my brother back and I love him for it. Unfortunately, it also means he hasn't visited me for a whole week. I try not to worry but given that all it takes for him to see me is to open a portal and pop in, it makes it weird that he hasn't spared five minutes to see me. At least to say hello. But nope. Nada. Zilch.

Who's annoyed? Not me.

I carefully remove the catheter and safely dispose of it, turning on my heel to head for the end table. "Do me a favor and help me clean him up while I jot down the notes."

"Certainly," Seth offers me a side smile showcasing his right dimple. I ignore it, despite the single butterfly fluttering in my stomach. Die butterfly. I have a boyfriend.

Crap . . . I'm missing his feeding checklist.

"So, lunch?"

"Uh . . . Sorry Seth, I brought my own today. Give me a moment to grab his checklist; this is the wrong one. I'll be right back. Are you okay to get him cleaned up?"

He nods at me and I head out of the hospital room to the desk outside. I quickly reach over to the other side, opening a drawer next to my coworker on the phone. I pull out the correct form and make my way to the room.

"Got it."

"That was quick." Seth finishes cleaning up our patient while I fill out the checklist when the heart rate monitor starts to speed up. That's unusual. I drop the paperwork and run to my patient's side.

"What happened?" I rush to check his vitals and make sure everything is properly attached. His breathing tubes are in place, everything is connected. What the hell is happening? Seth alerts the hospital staff and three more nurses come rushing in.

Sweat beads down my neck as a few seconds later, his heart rate flatlines and one of the nurses calls the time of death. I clutch my chest and swallow a breath. My heart skips a beat, sending an irregular vibrating thump through my body but I ignore it. I'm on medication and I'll survive. My patient didn't. They tell you not to get too close to your patients. But I'm only human. And this one meant something. I'm going to be the one to call his wife and explain to her that we lost him under my care. For reasons I can't understand. Where did I go wrong? I checked everything. I'm always extremely cautious. Unless something in the feeding tube was bad? No, that's impossible.

A gentle hand presses on my shoulder.

"I'm sorry Addison," Seth says.

"I know." A part of me half expects Ambrose to turn up now and be the one to comfort me, giving me one last chance to say goodbye to my patient. I flick my eyes around the room, hoping to see or hear those portal vents opening. I guess a different reaper took the job. Ambrose would be able to freeze time and let me be a part of it. Damnit, Ambrose. He knew how much this patient meant to me.

"You should take the rest of the day off," Seth says. "Let us take care of this."

"No, I can handle it."

"You sure?"

"It should be me."

He places his arm on mine and urges me out the door. "I think the doctor wants you to go home. There are plenty of us here who can do this." Seth lowers his voice to a whisper and his dark eyes pierce mine. "Go home, Addison. Call your boyfriend and don't be alone today."

Shit, when did Doctor Peters say that to him? Am I going to lose my job? Was this really my fault?

I swallow hard. "Don't think my boyfriend will be around today either but my dad's home." Seth creases his forehead with a sorry look on his face.

"I'll get out of your hair."

"Oh, Addison? Don't forget your medication at the front desk."

Flecainide, one dose to be taken every twelve hours. The air blowing out of my car's air conditioning turns from warm to cool on my face as I sit reading the instructions of my new medication. Just a few months ago, I had chalked my heart palpitations up to anxiety or stress. And then right after I opened a portal to the other side, I fainted. Luckily, I began working for a new doctor who can treat me. I've come to terms with my new condition and even though it isn't permanent, it makes me feel the weight of my mortality, as my mother had died from a heart attack. Apparently, heart conditions run in my family. And if anything were to happen to me, who would look after my father?

The car engine revs as I turn the key in the ignition. After today, cuddling with my boyfriend is the only thing in the world I want right now. And maybe a full glass of wine . . . or two. I can't believe I lost that patient. I inhale deeply, letting out broken breaths. It just doesn't make any sense . . . Ambrose is the only one who could make me feel better right now. I need him here, with me.

I place my hand on my necklace. All I need to do is hold it and think of him, and Ambrose will eventually come. At least that's what he told me when he gave it to me, but I never had to use it before, because he's usually good about visiting me. But now an entire week of trying has passed, and I haven't seen him. I shrug it off to him being busy and push down the feeling that there's something else keeping him.

I jump in my seat as a tapping on my driver's window breaks my concentration.

"Sorry Addison, I didn't mean to startle you. You forgot your credit card."

A hoarse chuckle escapes my throat and I lower the window, squinting through the sunlight to his dimpled grin and dark brown hair. "You're kidding me? I'd leave my head behind too if it weren't screwed on. Thanks so much Seth, you're a lifesaver."

He chuckles, giving me a playful smile. "Well, saving lives is the plan. So, do you and your man have any plans tonight?" he says, leaning into my window.

I raise an eyebrow. "Tonight?"

"You know, for Valentine's Day?" His attempt at hiding a chuckle puts a knot in my throat. I totally forgot about that stupid holiday. Especially with what just went wrong in the hospital, what could possibly make him think I want to celebrate? He should be torn up too. I bite my tongue. No, I need to learn how to separate work from home life. But still, I do wish for a quiet night with Ambrose.

"Oh, uh . . . we're not really a Valentine's Day type of couple," I say, swallowing hard, not wanting to explain that my reaper boyfriend probably doesn't even know what Valentine's Day is. "We do plenty of romantic things all the time. We don't need a holiday." Hopefully, that's enough to end the conversation.

"Uh huh . . . well my shift ends in two hours."

I stifle a sigh. Damn his persistence. Seth has dimples that could make a girl weak at the knees. Not me of course, because I have a boyfriend. But I'll be damned if he could take a hint. "I think I'm gonna just stay in. I have some reading to do anyway, sorry. Rain check?"

He gives me a lopsided smirk, still lingering into my driver's window. "Long-distance relationships can be tough. If he doesn't come around, why don't we have dinner and chill—as friends? No strings attached, as they say." Seth's deep brown eyes bore into mine. I avert my eyes, lowering them.

"Oh, I wasn't implying that you were trying to um . . . Right, okay how about I'll let you know if I can later?"

"Sounds good to me. I better get back to work." His muscles flex under his light green scrubs as he lifts himself up from my window. He gives me another sly smile as he turns and walks back inside the hospital.

I wave him off and drive home. I normally don't let Seth's flirting bother me because I always feel secure in my relationship with Ambrose. But something about today left me with an emptiness in the pit of my stomach. Being busy is one thing, but this really isn't like him at all. My cheeks burn up at the thought of me being the needy girlfriend waiting by the phone. He just isn't the type to be gone for days without popping in. It's Ambrose for Christ's sake. He doesn't play games, or understand them for that matter.

He can literally open a portal and walk into my bedroom at any time. But he hasn't. Of course, I can't explain this type of long-distance relationship to Seth. He isn't a magickal person. Even for a magickal person, my circumstance is particularly unique. I shake the feeling off. I'm being stupid. I probably only feel this way because it *is* stupid Valentine's Day, and I'm at home. Alone. Ambrose doesn't understand the passing of time for me. He probably wouldn't get why I'm uneasy about not hearing from him after only a week.

As usual, the mansion is freezing, and I welcome the blast of cold air conditioning after walking in from the South Florida heat. I set my purse down on a chair in the foyer and press the talk button on the intercom. "Dad, I'm home." Without waiting for a response, I start up the stairs when my father responds, "In the kitchen."

The rancid smell of stale coffee greets me as I pass a half-filled cup from early morning. "What are you eating?" I ask my father as I step over a pile of books on the floor.

"Oh, I'm just having a little snack. Do you want me to make you one?" Orlando spreads some of his homemade thyme butter on a cracker. The table is packed with books about sigils. For months he's had his head buried in his work, designing new sigils, attempting to refine masterful symbols for the most complex of spells. Sigils are created by combining scriptures or symbols and then imbuing them with a spellcaster's will. This way, the spell always works so long as it's drawn on something.

I scan some of the scribbled notes with coffee stains which, at this point, are illegible. "No thanks, I'll leave you to it. Dad, have you seen Ambrose or Dax today?"

Orlando shakes his head and pops another cracker in his mouth. "No, mi amor, my love, not today. I'm sorry."

I mask my disappointment with a smile. "Think I'll tend to my herb garden in a little while." I lean over and plant a kiss on his cheek before heading to my room. I throw myself on my bed and stare at my phone screen, mindlessly scrolling through my social media accounts. A loud unintentional sigh escapes my lungs and I let my phone drop on the bed with a soft thud. Closing my eyes, I twirl my pendant between my fingers, memorizing the curves of the glass flower Ambrose crafted for me. Before the night he gave this to me, I had never realized how he helped ease the pain of those that pass. Before bringing me back, he had taken me to his quarters in the astral plane, a place so different and peaceful, more beautiful than anywhere I have ever seen. A smile slides on my face as I reminisce. The night we danced together. I squeeze my eyes shut as I concentrate on the way his hair fell against his forehead, his crystal blue eyes that never left mine, and his gentle smile always made me weak every time I see it. I rub the flower pendant between my fingertips, hoping he will come in through a portal.

Two hours later I wake from a deep sleep. My frown deepens as I realize he never came. Where is he? I reach for my phone and check the time: seven o'clock. So much for my herb garden. I miss living with Ava. Despite me wanting to be close to my father, I miss being able to hang out with a friend. So now what? I'm just going to stay home and mope? Wish for my boyfriend to come through a portal?

I grab my phone again and stare at my address book. I really have been spending too much time with Seth recently. Not that Ambrose would mind me having a male friend. He isn't the jealous type. What's the harm? Fuck it, it's not like I can concentrate on anything productive. I dial his number.

Seth answers the phone without even so much as a hello. "Chinese food?"

I roll my eyes. "Sure."

"I'll be right over."

Thirty minutes later, I open the door for my friend. A strong blend of cologne and Chinese spices assault my nostrils as Seth shuts the door behind him.

"I can never get over how cool your house is. So different from the rest of the Keys." I shoot him a look as his eyes dart all over the room.

"Thanks, my dad designed it."

"He has great taste. Where should we eat?"

"Let's eat at the bar, I meant to check on my plants earlier but took a nap instead," I say, leading him through the Venetian room and into the bar area.

"Oh, and how are your little magical plants doing? Can they talk yet?"

"Hey, don't make fun of me. Our craft is serious business."

A dimple appears on Seth's cheek. "Don't worry, I find it cool. You're different from other women. I like that."

"And no flirting," I say, glaring at him. "I have a boyfriend."

A witty smile pastes on his face as he sets the food down on the bar and takes a seat on one of the stools. "I wasn't flirting."

"Mhmm." I quickly water my plants before sitting down next to him.

Seth stuffs a piece of chicken in his mouth. "Have you taken your medicine today?"

"I will before bed. Don't worry, I'm a nurse, I can take care of myself."

"Even nurses need help too sometimes."

"Is that right?"

He gives me another one of his crooked smiles with his mouth full of chicken as he chews. "So, did you talk to your boyfriend?"

I lower my eyes to my plate and shake my head. I really can't handle talking about Ambrose right now.

"That's not good. I'm sure he'll turn up," he says with his mouth full. "How can he not?"

I smile and nod. I'd rather change the subject to something else that is eating away at me. The tightness in my chest hasn't left since the hospital room. "Seth—I . . ." My voice cracks.

"What's the matter?"

He really doesn't seem bothered by this at all. "About today. Did I . . . do something? Was it my fault? Is it something I need to fess up to?" I gulp and stab a piece of chicken with my fork, not intending to eat it. My eyes water, and I quickly dry my tears.

"What? About your patient?" I close my eyes.

"Oh Addison." He cleans his hand off on a napkin before wrapping his arm around me, drawing me in close. Now I'm regretting bringing anything up. More so because I really do not want to cry on Seth's shoulders. "I'm really sorry. I should have realized how much that would break you. I guess from my days in the military, my walls are so high up I forget to bring them down sometimes. It affected me too; I just want you to know. And no. You are not at fault, and Dr. Peters knows that. Sometimes this just happens, okay?" He rubs my arm with his hand.

I'm about to answer when low venting comes from behind us. Goosebumps ripple down my spine and my heart flutters. I spin around in my chair and jump up. Ambrose? Oh shit!

How am I going to explain to Seth that my boyfriend just magickally appeared? I pull away from Seth's embrace and straighten myself up.

"We have a problem," a crisp woman's voice comes from the Venetian room and I grow pale in the face. I know that voice. A tall woman with straight red hair comes into view.

"Deacon? What are you doing here? Where's Ambrose?"

"Uh, what's going on? Where'd *you* come from?" Seth jumps up from the stool and looks behind Deacon to check for a doorway. The portal Deacon stepped out of quickly closes behind her and I slap myself in the forehead. Shit.

"Woah, what the hell *was* that?" Seth asks.

Shit. Shit. Shit!

Deacon flashes a look at Seth and then back to me.

"Believe me, Addison, I wouldn't have come here if it wasn't an emergency. Ambrose is in danger."

The blood drains from my face. Woah. I was not expecting that. "What do you mean? How can he be in danger?" My voice quivers.

"Wait," Seth interrupts. "Who's in danger? Are we just going to ignore the fact that this woman just stepped out of a black hole in the corner of the room?"

Deacon ignores him. "He was abducted by demons and now I cannot find him anywhere. I just thought you should know."

Just thought I should know? My heart slams in my chest and the room starts to spin. I grab on to my head. This doesn't make any sense. Then my heart sinks. "Wait, where's my brother? How can this happen? Reapers don't just go missing!"

"Demons? Reapers? Who's in danger?" Seth's voice rises with each question, his eyes darting from me to Deacon. "Will someone tell me what the hell is going on?"

Deacon's usually expressionless face contorts. "Your brother is missing too."

"Woah wait, they're *both* missing?" My knees grow weak. Sure as hell I'm about to faint. I stumble over to a chair near the door and hold my stomach; afraid I might lose my dinner.

"Addison, this is really serious. There is something terribly wrong. I only came here to tell you, but I must go now. I have to find them."

How can this even be possible? What would be strong enough to abduct Ambrose? The strange note with the astral rose I found on my nightstand on Christmas Day emerges in my mind. I get an icky feeling in the pit of my stomach. When I had told Ambrose about it, he said he would ask around. But he came back saying the Akashic waters were even checked, but nothing showed up. "No, wait. Let me come with you." I stammer, getting to my feet.

Seth grabs my arm. "Go with her where? Through that glowing thing? Okay, everyone stop. Addison, what the hell is going on?"

I draw back and glance a watery eye at Seth. "It's called a portal. I'm sorry. You need to leave. My boyfriend and brother are in trouble and I need to go look for them."

"What? What do you mean? Does she mean *demons*, like in the movies?"

I raise an eyebrow and give him a slight shrug.

Seth puts his palms over his eyes. "Are you people saying that your boyfriend is a reaper? Like, the *Grim Reaper*?"

"Not the Grim Reaper, just a reaper. There are many," Deacon says. "Addison, I cannot let you come with me. Ambrose would not be pleased with me. I must go alone."

"Deacon, please. I won't be able to stay here knowing that my brother and boyfriend are in danger."

Deacon opens her mouth to speak but Seth interjects. "Wait," Seth interrupts. "You're going through a portal with this woman? To where? Are you insane?"

I drop my hands and sigh. "Seth, you wouldn't understand."

"Hell no, Addison. And without any weapons? Like, you're just going to go off into another dimension? I must be dreaming. This isn't really happening. Is this really happening?"

My eyes light up. "Seth, you're a genius!" I turn to Deacon. "I'll take my dagger."

Deacon stares at me for a moment. "Fine. Hurry up and get it. We don't have much time."

I shoot up and nearly slam into the door. "I'll be fast." I

crane my neck just as I step through the doorway. "Seth, you really need to leave."

"Oh, I'm not going anywhere. This is all totally crazy. First of all, I can hardly believe any of this is real. I mean, I know you said you practiced magick but . . ."

I let him trail off as I dash up the stairs to get to my room. I go into my closet and open up a wooden box I keep hidden. My eyes widen as I hold the empty box in my hand. "It's gone."

"What's gone?" Seth and Deacon caught up with me in my bedroom.

"A powerful dagger that my father gave to me. He said it would always keep me safe. But it's gone." And I really need to stop blurting things about magick to Seth. I never minded him knowing I practiced, but there's a limit to what I should say to non-magick folk.

"Maybe your father has it?" Seth asks.

"No, he would never take something from my room without asking. And he wouldn't need my—"

"The dagger is gone? Stolen?" Deacon cuts me off.

My head fogs and I pinch my crinkled forehead. "No, that's impossible. No one ever comes in here."

"Something strange is happening, Addison. Two reapers get ambushed, now your dagger is missing. You cannot come without it. I can't promise I can protect you. Whatever it was that took Ambrose and Dax could probably take me too, make no mistake about that." The dim room light reflects off her red hair, giving her an ethereal allure.

My eyes narrow at Deacon, keeping a stern lip. "I'm still going. Especially if my dagger has been stolen. I need to get to the bottom of this."

Deacon sighs. "We're not sure if it was stolen, but if it *was*, and it is somewhere around the astral plane, then you will not be able to bring it back to this dimension without a crane bag."

"What the fuck is a crane bag?" Seth yells. I flick my gaze up toward him. "You're still here? This doesn't involve you. Deacon, yes, you're right. My father keeps it hidden away in his room. Wait for me here while I go get it. I have to be quiet. I don't want him knowing about any of this. The last thing I need my father to do is worry."

Pages ruffle from inside the library doors. My father has moved back into the library to continue his work. Even though he is a great sorcerer, he is known to get worked up over his children and make grave mistakes. I make it up to my father's room and silently turn the handle. He keeps a safe inside a trapdoor in my mother's closet. I open the closet doors wide and can still smell my mother's old perfume on the clothes. My father likes to keep all her stuff exactly as it was. I crouch down and move some shoe boxes out of the way. The combination to the safe is my mother's birthday. I successfully open the heavy metal door and find a little blue box. Inside is a leather bag with fur so black, it shines blue—a reflection of its power. My father once said he had taken it from an astral realm. It was the only way anyone could bring a magickal item from that world to this one. Whoever stole the dagger must have had one as well.

A chill zips up my spine and my stomach churns. This means someone was in my room. Yuck. Who the hell has been here?

I have never heard of demons being able to ambush reapers. Even back when Ozo was tormenting me and my father, Ambrose was still able to use his scythe on him. A sinking feeling overcomes me. What if it wasn't a demon, but another reaper?

Deep in thought, I open the door, with little pressure on the handle to avoid it creaking too loud. I come face to chest with a man standing in front of me and almost jump out of my skin. "Damnit Seth, I told you to go home."

"I'm not letting you go through a portal and off into some kind of Narnia. There's no way."

I push him out of my way. "I'm not asking you for permission. I have to do this. Who do you think you are? You're not my father or my boyfriend." Not that I would let Ambrose tell me what to do either, but that's beside the point.

"No, but I don't think your boyfriend would respect me much if I let you walk headfirst into danger either."

"You don't know my boyfriend. He's a pretty logical guy. He can understand my worries."

"Yeah well, this isn't logical."

Just as I'm about to reply, something smacks into the window.

"Crowley!" I squint at him through the glass.

The owl shakes his feathers and inspects the three of us with accusing, large eyes. I approach the window to let him in, but he lets out a soft screech and takes off. I shrug and shake my head.

"I'm going with you," Seth says.

"Absolutely not." Deacon, who is standing at the foot of the stairs, answers for me.

"Addison, I'm not letting you do this alone. If what," Seth looks over at Deacon, "she says is true, then I'm sure your brother and boyfriend had to put up a fight. If they were ambushed, I mean. You know I was in the army. I was an infantry commander. Let me at least *try* to protect you. Not to mention, magickal portal! I can't pass this up." His eyes widen into a puppy dog plea.

"Seth, I appreciate you wanting to look after me, but no amount of training could prepare you for what might be out there. Your military training is no good here."

"Right, I doubt that." Seth huffs and folds his arms.

"It's time to go. You stay back, mortal," Deacon says as she opens the portal.

"Wait, let me write my dad a note." I run back into my room and take out a pen and paper.

Dad, I'll be back soon.

Love, Addison.

Cold air chills my skin as it blows out of the portal. I reach into my closet and grab a cloak, and my medication, stashing it in the crane bag. "Okay, I'm ready."

Deacon opens the portal back up. "After you."

"Addison . . ." Seth starts.

Ignoring him, I turn my back and step into the portal, with Deacon close behind me. Turning back, I catch a glimpse of Seth jumping in right before the portal closes.

Idiot.

THE AXEMAN

ADDISON

"I cannot believe you followed us into the astral plane after I told you to go home." I grit my teeth, angry but also to keep them from chattering from the icy atmosphere from the astral plane. My face reddens as I stand facing Seth with my arms crossed out in front of me. My heart races. I ball my fist as he tries not to smile. The nerve of him!

"I told you I wasn't going to let you waltz into some dimension or whatever without me."

The calmness in his tone unnerves me even more. "Who the hell do you think you are? You're not my keeper. What do you mean by *let me*? No one *lets* me do anything. I do what I want, and if that means me going to find my brother and boyfriend in an astral dimension then so be it."

Seth smacks the sides of his jeans. "Will you please calm down? I'm here already."

"No, Deacon, send him back please," I say, turning to face Deacon, who is patiently letting me rip Seth a new one.

"No, Deacon, please don't. I promise I'll make myself useful," Seth says, before Deacon can get a word in.

Deacon raises her chin and lets out a short shake, making her form turn back to a skeleton draped in a long black cloak. I resist a shudder and bite my lip. It's a sight I will never get used to.

"We can use him," Deacon says.

"What? How?" I spin on my heel to face Deacon.

"I have a feeling I'll know how when the time comes. For now, we must stop wasting time. There's a lot of ground to cover."

Great. We're stuck babysitting a complete newbie to this world. I pull my cloak tighter around my shoulders and take a deep breath. Mist covers our legs as I scan our surroundings. The only thing lighting our path is a subtle glow from the horizon creeping over the tall, ruined archways. This is one place in the astral dimension I have never been to. If I'm honest, outside of Ambrose's personal quarters, and my dad's pocket dimension at home, I haven't travelled too far out. I glaze over gargoyle-like images etched into the dark grey stonework.

Goosebumps prick my arms. Just like the first time I walked into the astral in my physical state from my father's library portal, it is freezing. I glance at Seth and shake my head disapprovingly. "Fine, I guess we're just wasting time arguing. Stay close, there's a lot for you to learn and I don't need you getting lost."

Seth smirks. "Yes, ma'am."

"Both of you stay close to me," Deacon spits. "You *both* can get lost."

"I won't get lost," I say, picking up the pace. "What's the plan anyway? Where are we going?"

Deacon hesitates. "The plan is to find Ambrose—"

The floor shakes. Starting out as a rumble, getting

stronger by the minute. Rocks come crashing down the pillars and I hit the floor as a jolt erupts beneath our feet. I get back to my feet and Deacon quickly grabs mine and Seth's arms, pushing us behind her. Dark burgundy clouds surface above our heads; lightning strikes between them. The images of demons in the walls move before my eyes, demons etched and unmoving open their jaws, in a screaming stretch. Some flee, while others carry on their tasks of torturing souls. I wince as one pushes a talon into another's back and rips out their spine.

My head spins; my stomach lurches. I fall back to my knees, my arm still being held by Deacon's bony hand.

My heart thuds out of rhythm. I reach for my crane bag. Although there isn't any time for me to take my medicine, making sure it's still there gives me comfort.

In between the clouds, a large, horned demon cloaked in crimson rides out on a white, winged steed. His voice bellows in my ears, making me wince.

"What are you doing here?" His eyes move between us as his steed gallops between the clouds.

I struggle to stand, but Seth grips me hard enough for me to regain my balance. He moves in front of me, trying to be the hero. I try pushing him to the side but he pushes me back.

"Are you the asshole who assaulted my brother and boyfriend?" I bark from over Seth's shoulder.

"Uh, Addison? What are you doing?" Seth says.

The demon grimaces but doesn't say a word. He takes a moment to inspect each of us as his steed trots in front of us, causing strong winds to offset our footing. He slows until his steed stops in front of Deacon.

His crimson eyes reflect off the lighting from the clouds he brought with him. He lifts a hand and points it at her.

Deacon takes out her scythe and points it at him faster than he lets out a flash of red lightning.

Lightning hits right next to my feet and Seth pushes me back, sending us both lunging off to the ground. My skin scrapes against the rough, cold surface of the stone floor. We scramble to our knees, using each other to keep our balance. Thick fog assaults my nostrils, making it hard to breathe as I dart my eyes around the dark corridor. Where's Deacon? I couldn't see what happened after the lightning hit.

Shit! Where the fuck did she go? "What did you do to her?" I say, turning to the demon who has jumped off his steed.

I struggle to pull my gaze away from the horns that twist toward the back of his head. His dark eyes size me up from top to bottom. A glint of hunger sparks in them as he drinks in every detail of me, like he's undressing me with his eyes.

I want to sink into my own skin, get out of dodge but I fight it. I need answers. I swallow as he locks eyes with me and moves in slowly, calm, collected, calculated. My stomach knots as a lightning strike illuminates his toned biceps as he saunters toward me.

"Your friend left you here to fend for yourself."

I flick my eyes toward Seth but no longer see him. It's too dark and this demon is blocking my view.

Dryness scratches at my throat as I try to speak. "D–Deacon?"

"But don't worry," he says. "I will find her."

I move back as he continues to inch toward me. The wall meets my back and I have nowhere to go. "W–what do you want with the reapers? Do you have my boyfriend?"

He curls up his full lips, giving me a side smirk. A

dimple shows up on his cheek, reminding me of Seth. I hope he's alright.

"I do."

"And my brother?" I stammer.

He smiles but doesn't answer. His deep gaze searches my eyes and makes my knees quiver. His silence is deafening. What's he playing at?

"Why are you here, Addison Castillo?"

"H—how do you know my name?" Stupid question. He just admitted to having Ambrose and Dax.

He lifts a finger and slides it down my cheek, lowering his face close enough to brush my cheek bone. "Oh, I know all about you, Addison." His breath is deep and steady.

My eyes widen . . . "Were you the one w—who . . . left a note in my room?"

He gives me another smug lip curl but just stands there, studying me in the uneasy silence. What is he doing?

"I've been waiting to meet you for a very, very long time." His voice is low and smooth, cracking at the start of his words. Almost sexy if he wasn't so intimidating.

"W—why?" I mutter.

"I need your help."

"My help? What could I possibly do to help you?"

He lifts his chin, his eyes towering over me from his tall stature. "A long time ago, I hid a dagger where it could never be found so that it wouldn't fall in the hands of a very entitled reaper."

"Ambrose?"

"No, not Ambrose."

"Then who?"

"That's not important, you don't know this reaper. What he failed to realize was that I always have a fail-safe. That dagger was entrusted to your family. I had it sent to be protected by someone who has demon blood. A product of light and dark magick."

I draw my brows together . . . What does this have to do with me? The soft lighting from the corridors outline the sharp edges of his features as he looms over me.

"I needed my keys, my weapons, to release me from my prison. I couldn't have done it without my spies."

"What's any of this got to do with me?"

"Your dagger is *mine*. And it's a key to open up my father's cage. Only you, Addison, can open it."

"What? My dagger? How? I don't even have it . . . I—" I glower my eyes at him. "You stole it!"

"Technically, I retrieved it. But yes, I have it."

"If it's yours, then how is it only I can use it?"

"I didn't say only you could use it. I said only you could open my father's cage."

"But why?"

"After so many years, it has become a part of you. It responds to your blood. Your half light and dark blood. The lock needs your blood to open it."

"I don't under—"

"The reapers never thought a human like you would ever be possible. But I had to believe it. I just had to be patient."

My heart thuds . . . "If I open the cage to release your father. Will you let Ambrose go?"

He takes one step back and lifts his chin. "I will."

"And my brother?" He leans his head to the side and he looks me up and down again. I swallow.

"Yes. Do we have a deal?"

"And the rest of the reapers?" I might as well ask, right?

"No." His upper lip curls. "Those are mine."

They're not my problem anyway. But still . . . Something's not right. "H–how do I know you're telling me the truth?"

"As a show of good faith, I will let you have conjugal visits with your reaper."

"Well, why can't we go now?"

"You will have to prove your worth to the Akashic waters. I cannot take you."

Prove my worth? And all this to help him . . . ? "W–who is your father?"

"Don't concern yourself with semantics. Just know, he is the greatest light bearer there ever was. And he will make my home," he waves his arms, "all this, a much better place."

I gulp. Light bearer huh? There's only one "light bearer" I've ever heard of. "You don't mean . . . Lucifer?"

His facial expression hardens, his smug smirk wiping off his face. He tilts his head slightly and his eyes narrow. "Do we have a deal?"

Shit. If he wants me to release the freaking devil, I can't do it. There's no way in hell. But . . . I need to save my brother and Ambrose. I'll let him think I will, until I can figure something out.

"Deal."

The ground rumbles again and he grins. "Perfect."

"When can I see him?"

"Morticia?" His steed trots behind him and as quick as the tornado had formed, he jumps on his steed and rides off, disappearing into the red clouds.

A gust of air escapes my lungs and I place a hand on my panting chest. My knees quiver as everything starts to spin. Uh oh . . . please don't pass out. My eyes glaze over the walls as some of the etched demons look down at me, gaping, as they freeze back into place.

Seth runs to my aid and lowers me to sit on the

ground. He reaches into my crane bag, pulling out my meds. "Here, let me help you."

I nod, my hands still shaking. "He didn't say when . . ." I mutter under my breath.

"Don't worry about that now," Seth says. I look up at him and catch his eyes in the soft lighting from the top of the corridors. He winks at me and smiles. "I got you," he whispers. He opens the medicine bottle and shakes two pills into my hand.

I appreciate his kindness and take the medicine, one pill at a time, forcing myself to swallow without water. I hold on to my mouth, tears welling up at the corners of my eyes. It's hard enough for me to swallow pills with water, let alone dry. I've never been good at taking pills. I've always blamed it on my damn fear of suffocation. I tilt my head up and swallow the other one, puke rising in my stomach, but I swallow it down. My breath is heavy. I give myself a few moments before I can go on. "Where did you go?" I ask.

"I couldn't move, Addie. He had me pinned to a wall. I couldn't even see you. All I saw were red clouds . . ."

"Oh my gosh, Seth, I'm so sorry. You shouldn't have come. He could have killed you."

Seth holds my hand. "I was frightened. But not as much as I was seeing you jump into a portal, not knowing if you'd be okay, or if I'd ever see you again."

My chest tightens as I catch a glimpse of wetness in his eyes. He clears his throat and straightens up, lending me a sturdy hand. I take it as he helps me back up to my feet.

"Now, where to go from here . . . Without Deacon, I . . ." I let my words trail off and hold my breath as the demon's voice echoes in my mind, telling me she abandoned us.

"I'm here, Addison." My lungs release a big breath as Deacon's voice comes from the shadows.

"Deacon! You're okay! Where'd you go . . . I thought you . . ."

"Left?" Deacon's high cheekbones come into view as the mauve lighting bounces off of her. "No. Do you know who that was?"

"I have an idea who he is . . . He is the one who ambushed Ambrose and my brother."

"That was Azazel, Addison. I couldn't let him take me. You need me if we're going to save Ambrose."

"No, I know . . . I'm not mad at you. I'm glad you're safe." So, this confirms it then. He's the one who left me a note. "How come he wasn't able to take you?"

"Azazel was the first reaper. I share a telepathic connection. I can access the Akashic waters quicker than anyone else. I saw his attack moments before it happened."

That's right. I did know Deacon was psychic. I had just forgotten. It had never occurred to me she was more special than the other reapers. Ambrose told me she was next in line to the Judge's mantle, so I guess that makes her older. Do reapers develop powers? Or just Deacon? I suppose it is somewhat strange Ambrose has empathy . . . Maybe that actually is his power.

Deacon lowers her head, searching my gaze. "I am sorry I left you, Addison. Unfortunately, when I flung myself, only nearby to be close enough to watch you, Azazel had an ambush ready for me. I was able to fight them off, but they managed to take my scythe." Deacon holds her hands out. "We're unprotected now."

My eyes widen. "Holy fuck. They took your scythe? How did you get back?"

"I didn't land far. I was just in another room within the walls. I really am sorry."

"Don't be. I'm not hurt. We just . . . talked." I brush my hair away from my eyes.

"What did you guys talk about?" Seth says.

I ran them through what was discussed but before I could finish by saying I agreed, Seth jerks back. "Are you sure his father is the devil? Like, the actual fucking devil?"

"He didn't say. He said he was "the greatest light bearer and would make this place better."

"Sounds like the devil to me."

"Fat chance of me letting him out though. He was caged up for a reason. How could he make this place better?"

Seth's facial features harden as he gazes back at me. "So, what are you going to do?"

"We're going to keep going. He promised me conjugal visits with Ambrose as long as I help him. Out of good faith, he said. Then, he promised to release him and my brother after I open the gate."

"Great, let's get going." Deacon says.

"Well, the only problem is. He didn't say when." My blood curdles at the next thought. "He said something about having to prove myself."

Deacon spreads out her skeletal hands. "We'll think of something."

Seth rolls his eyes "So, conjugal huh?"

My cheeks redden.

"At least you'll get to have sex with your boyfriend while you're here."

"It's just visitation . . ."

"Yeah, whatever. He's your boyfriend. Do whatever you guys . . . do."

"It's really none of your business." Is he seriously acting jealous now? Has he already forgotten why we're here? And it is only visitation. I can't think about sex now.

Besides, Ambrose and I haven't even reached that stage of our relationship yet.

"Whatever. Can we go?" I turn to Deacon. "What's the plan? Wait around till I'm given"—I pause and snap a look at Seth—"visitation?" Seth rolls his eyes and I ignore him.

"No, we should keep going and head to the Akashic level. We will hopefully be able to get answers once there. If you do get to see Ambrose in the meantime, assuming Azazel keeps his promise, then you will be able to gather intel from Ambrose himself."

My stomach flutters at the idea of actually being able to see him. "Sounds like a plan. How far is the Akashic level?"

"Far since we need to travel by foot."

I scrunch up my features.

"Just stay close." Deacon says. We start walking and Seth trails off a few paces behind me.

"Hurry up," I snap at him, craning my neck. "What are you looking at?"

"These images . . . They're, pretty fucking awesome."

I grimace as my eyes stop at a picture of a bald creature, with large, presumably hollow eyes, and an elongated jaw, as if it's screaming. Patches or holes are etched all over its naked body. I'd rather if one not come to life on the wall. "They're grotesque."

I lock my eyes straight ahead as my surroundings darken. Shit, I can barely see Deacon anymore. I speed up, worried about losing sight of her. Getting lost in this place is the last thing I want. Water soaks the bottom of my jeans as I trudge ahead. What sounds like a leaky faucet drips in the distance. My eyes narrow at the mist covering my feet and I lift a leg up.

"Are we walking into water? I didn't know there was

water in the astral plane," my voice echoes and Deacon doesn't answer. "Deacon?" I stop in my tracks.

The only sound I hear is the sound of the drip, drip, drip of water somewhere near. I stick out my hand to see if I can feel Seth walking behind me and hopefully stop him, but there is no one there. Shit. We got separated.

"Seth? Deacon? Hello?" I tread on a little further— deeper into the water. "Where are you guys?" How the hell did we get separated? We were right behind each other. Son of a bitch! The last time this happened was when Dax and I walked into the library portal back home. Back then, I didn't know why that happened, but now looking back, it was because since Dax was dead. He wasn't allowed out of the confines of his house. I call out for them again, but my voice bounces off the walls.

Okay, stay focused and don't panic. We were walking in a straight line. If I keep going, I'm bound to run into Deacon again and then we can find Seth. I spin around. The only problem is, I can't remember which way we were headed. I call their names one more time and listen. Crap. Nothing but the dripping echoes through the mist. I walk toward the dripping sound, splashing through the water with my feet.

As I walk, the corridors widen, and the area thickens in darkness. The soft light that was barely illuminating the path is now gone. I slow my pace. I can't see shit. I stick a hand out but there are no walls, no borders, just darkness. The air is dry and cold, and the tip of my nose is frozen. A dim light flashes in the distance.

"Deacon? Is that you? Seth?"

The light flickers and then turns off, but no one answers. What was that? It couldn't have been Deacon. She doesn't have her scythe anymore, and even still, it would glow blue.

"Who's out there?" I mutter, my voice a lot lower than I had planned.

I stop walking. There could be other beings around, although from what I know of the astral plane, they would all be mental beings, creatures, egregores crafted by my own mind from whenever I was angry or sad. Dryness scratches my throat as I swallow.

A light flickers again, for a bit longer. "Seth? Is that you?"

The light flicks again for a few seconds, this time closer. Shaking, I take a step forward. A dark mass sweeps around me and a cold chill swivels up my spine. I hold my breath. It's not Deacon nor Seth. They would have answered. I spin around to see a long, cloaked figure.

"Who are you?" I stammer.

My skin crawls as something brushes my arm.

I stumble back and the once flickering light shines itself right on me. It isn't a cloak at all. It has burned, dried up skin hanging off its long, drooping face. Its hollow eyes burrow into mine, stretching its mouth until it almost reaches the floor. It floats high up above me and I make a run for it. What the hell is that? That came from my mind?

I run until I hit a wall and land backward on the wet ground with a damp thud. Rubbing the back of my head, I sit up, perplexed that there is now a wall when I thought I had veered off to some borderless area. As I move to stand, something lets out a terrifying moan. My eyes search around for the floating burned creature and see it shrinking off into the dark abyss. Dread seeps into my stomach. Why would it leave? Not because of me, surely . . . I place a hand on the wall, easing myself up off the ground. Steadying myself, I catch my reflection on a glinting blade in front of me. I gasp as I follow my eyes up a long ax hilt to the wielder. I suck in my breath, struggling to keep it steady. The hand around the hilt is at the height of my chest. This son of a bitch is tall, the tallest man I have ever seen. The figure wears a long, ragged cape behind a body of armor. He has a horned head, a long, wide, pointed nose, and no eyes. I wince as he moves his head down and opens his mouth, showing long, sharp, pointed teeth.

I move to make a dash but stumble backward and trip. I attempt to stand up and run at the same time. Finally, pulling myself together, I run back against the direction of the wall I had hit. I glimpse behind me. The blind axman is still walking toward me, swinging his ax from side to side.

I crouch low into the mist, watching as the axman stands there, waiting for me to move. There is nowhere for me to go. This guy is going to fucking kill me if I move. The axman turns around. Here's my chance. I run as fast as I can into the darkness with my hands out in front of me.

I reach another wall. Is it the same wall? Have I been going around in circles? A low moaning comes from behind me. I slowly turn around and come face-to-face with the burned-faced-creature I had run into before. "Stop it, leave me alone!" It gargles something back, but I can't make out what it's saying. Then something to my right grabs my wrist with dry wrinkly hands. Another burned monster with hollowed eyes!

"Don't touch me! Get away!" I shriek. The sound of steel clashing against stone sets me on edge. It's the blind axman walking toward us. The burned creatures groan as they grab for me. I back up against the wall as the crea- tures lengthen in size and press their faces up to mine. One of them reaches out and clamps its hand over my mouth. I wince, moving my head from side to side. "Let me go," I try to say but my words come out muffled. They're trying to suffocate me!

I try kicking them off, but they're strong as hell. The sound of the ax being dragged on the floor grows louder, competing with the sound of my own pulse growing louder in my eardrums.

The axman creeps up behind the creatures and swings his ax up high. I squeeze my eyes shut. I'm trapped.

LABYRINTH

ADDISON

*M*y chest heaves under the frigid clasp of the burned ones. I don't know what's worse: their scratchy grip or the smell of rotting flesh making me want to gag. Their grip releases me. I draw my hands in and open one eye to see the double-edged ax chopping their heads clean off their loosely fleshed bodies. I wince as they each make a splash on the cold damp floor. I press my back against the stone wall as the axman stands inches from my face. I draw in my breath, trying not to make a sound, swallowing hard as my heart skips a beat. Please don't see me. Please don't see me. How *can* he without any eyes?

The giant brings up his ax and reaches far behind him. My eyes widen and a small gasp escapes my throat.

As the ax comes down, something pulls me to the right.

I muffle a scream, thinking it's another burnt one coming back for me.

"Come on, this way!"

Seth?

He grabs my hand and guides me to an open entrance

within the wall. "We're safe here." I lean back against the wall, catching my breath. "How'd you find me?"

Deacon emerges from the shadows, holding up a lantern. "I found him first and brought him here."

"Was that you guys earlier? I kept seeing a light, but it kept disappearing. I thought it was one of those things out there."

Seth crouches down next to me. "It was us. I kept calling out your name, but you couldn't hear us. Then when they surrounded you Deacon showed me a way through the walls."

I climb to my feet, forcing my eyes to make out the features of the room. "So, this is what Deacon meant when she said she went to a nearby room. Where'd the lantern come from?"

Seth shrugs.

"What were those things?"

"The burned ones are lost souls. There are many more out there in different forms," Deacon says, emerging from the shadows.

"I thought they wanted to kill me. But then that axe man chopped their heads off."

"It really depends on who they were in life and what happened to them. Some of them are just confused and looking for help, others will do you harm."

"What about the axe man?" I say, still out of breath. I gaze up at Deacon's face, the light from the lantern high-lighting her sharp cheekbones.

"That was a guardsman. They clear out the lost wandering throughout the level. Keep anything from getting into the Akashic realm."

"A guardsman? Are there more of them?"

"Yes, this place is swarming with guards. It's why I told

you to keep close. They can smell a spirit of any kind. Fear too, and you probably reek of it," she spits.

"Well, of course I do. It's a giant with horns, wielding an ax." My heart is still pumping adrenaline. I put my hand on the crane bag I had tied onto my belt loop, making sure it didn't fall loose during my encounter.

"Creatures here that have no eyes see differently. They're kind of psychic, if you will. Are we ready to keep going?"

"So, what? If they don't need eyes, they won't have them?"

"Precisely."

"Hold on. Aren't we still in the astral level? I thought the only creatures I would see are my own egregores? Did we take a shortcut? Where are we?"

Seth tugs at my arm. "Deacon explained everything to me while we were trying to find you. Apparently, this place is like a pitch-black labyrinth. We're getting close to the mental plane and as we near the Akashic realm, the halls are guarded."

I take a deep breath. Ambrose never explained how any of the realms worked. But it's not like he would expect me to go roaming around here on my own anyway. I turn to face Deacon.

"Can you draw me a map of the realms, please? I'm confused. Why were we in the astral plane for such a short amount of time? And what's in the mental plane? And what's with the water? Deacon, where are we exactly?"

Deacon glances at Seth then looks back at me. "The water means we're getting close to the realm of knowledge. Hence the word *Akashic*." She lets out a heavy sigh. "We're in LLAPS—"

"Laps? What is that?"

Deacon purses her lips. "LLAPS stands for 'lower level of the astral planes.'"

My eyes widen. "Lower level? Is that like hell? Are we in *hell*?"

"No. We don't have time for this. Let's keep going, I'll explain on the way."

Her words make my stomach twist. Something doesn't feel right. "Fine, lead the way."

Deacon starts walking but talks to us at the same time. "The mental plane meets the fifth dimension in certain areas of the labyrinth. The only reason why you get to see your nightmares come to life, emanating your past emotions, or conflict, is because your dimension lies close to the mental plane. That's where all memories from your subconscious get stored. Like a giant web of emotions, connecting everyone, and every creature. The astral dimension comprises all of the planes. If your dimension were close to, say, the Akashic, then more humans would be psychic. Do you understand?"

My eyes widen. It makes perfect sense.

Deacon continues, "The mental plane can be a beautiful place. But you have to be careful when we get to it. Even though it's full of your egregores, your deep and darkest emotions, and you can bring your imagination to life there, nefarious dwellers still live there."

"Demons?"

"No, not demons. Just other beings who are from there. Some aren't bad. Just stay close to me at all times."

"The mental plane sounds cool," Seth chimes in.

I lick my chapped lips as hot air hits my face. A brutal contrast to what it felt like when we first got here. I follow behind Deacon, with Seth closely behind me. He seems to be trotting along happily. I would have expected him to be a lot more frightened. I suppose it was exciting. "I never thought it would get hot out here."

"The temperature varies," Deacon says. "Just like it does in your world."

"It really *is* like a labyrinth, isn't it?" Seth says.

"Oh yeah, I guess it is. Like one long, dark maze." I try giving him a smile as I glance back but it's too dark. We keep a brisk pace, but I step over to the side to walk next to him. I had shouted at him all night. True, he had followed me in here to keep me safe, but what kind of a match would he be against a demon? Especially when I have a reaper on my side? In spite of myself though, I do appreciate him.

"Fun fact," he says as I walk beside him, "a maze has many different pathways and entrances, leading to more than one exit, while a labyrinth has only one path. It leads out to a center, and then back out the same way you started from."

I squint through the darkness. "I never knew that. I guess we have been going in one direction since we got here. Maybe this really is a labyrinth." What are the chances I'll run into the goblin king? One could only get so lucky . . . I smirk to myself.

"Well, technically, using a portal was cheating but since we don't have that option right now, onward through the black stone walls!"

He shows his teeth when he smiles. I let out a chuckle. "Lead the way."

Deacon interrupts from ahead of us, "Follow me, I definitely know the way . . ."

Seth and I exchange a glance and laugh. A soft glow comes in and out of view as we walk deeper into these corridors and I catch a glimpse of Seth's dimples. My cheeks warm and I dart my eyes straight ahead. Lights ahead grow closer. It would be nice to finally be able to see where we're going, but the lights are sporadic and dim.

As we get nearer, glowing sigils light the dark stone pathway. These sigils glow like fire but they don't burn when I step on them. Passing a few of them, I recognize some of them are Enochian symbols while others are sigils with a mixture of different scriptures. Some runes entwined with Egyptian hieroglyphs, some with Babylonian.

"Strange."

"What's that?" Seth asks.

"These symbols on the ground. I didn't think ancient scriptures from our world would be found here. Wouldn't the . . . creatures here have their own language?" I wince at my choosing of the word *creatures*. Inhabitants? I've definitely seen creatures, but I know there are different levels of demons. I mean, especially by the looks of these sigils.

Deacon sighs but doesn't look back. "There are different worlds connected by the astral plane. But you'll find scriptures known to all here. With language comes power, and everything becomes permanent here first."

"Well, it does make sense if you think about it," Seth adds. "Aren't we all meant to be connected to the astral planes by our subconscious? And Enochian was invented by Edward Kelly and John Dee as a form of communication to what they thought were angels. So, why wouldn't all scriptures be here?"

I scrunch up my features and narrow my eyes at him. "First of all, John Dee and Kelly did not *invent* the Enochian scriptures, it was taught to them *by* the Enochian angels. And secondly, how do you know so much about the planes and how we're connected? I thought you didn't *believe* in this stuff."

"Well, first, I just met a grim reaper and walked

through a portal. Belief is in the eye of the beholder and I just beheld. Second, I took a philosophy class in college," he says, giving me that sly smile of his.

"Right, okay." I guess that makes sense. Maybe he's not as much of a tool as I thought he was. More and more symbols burn bright on the ground and are now emerging on the walls and floating overhead. "That's beautiful."

"It is pretty stunning isn't it?" Seth says. I flick a gaze toward him and he's staring right at me.

As we walk, I fixate on the emblems all around me, trying to identify which symbols I recognize, and which ones I've never seen before, trying to see if I could decipher them. Are they wards? Or are they just different spells? I spin around momentarily to see the symbols disappearing into the distance. I reach out and pass my hand through one of them to see what would happen. They move between my fingers like smoke.

Seth laughs. "What are you doing?"

I crack a smile. "Just wanted to see what would happen."

Seth joins me, weaving his hands through the symbols. He grins back at me and my cheeks flush. I bring my hands down, remembering why we're here. To rescue my boyfriend. My heart sinks to the pit of my stomach as guilt chokes my throat for allowing myself to laugh and blush at Seth.

Seth's eyes soften in the glow of the symbols; he must have sensed the shift in my mood. "Can I ask you a question?"

"Sure, what's up?"

"So, your boyfriend is a reaper, right?"

"Yes."

"Well, I guess we can't control who we fall in love with but . . ."

I raise an eyebrow. "But?"

"Well, I don't know. Don't you ever think about having a family? The white picket fence and all?"

"Excuse me?"

"What I'm trying to ask is, do you ever think about wanting kids? I mean, can a reaper have children? Isn't he, I don't know, dead? What kind of life would that be?"

My lips part slightly as my stomach turns. I hadn't put too much thought into having children with Ambrose. Life with him feels so eternal, despite my condition, and me feeling my mortality all the time. I guess he makes me forget. I place my hand on my chest, the constant reminder of my mortality. My heart has skipped beats several times since we followed Deacon through the portal.

"Does he age? What happens when you get old and he still looks the same?"

My head starts to spin. "I um . . ." I shut my eyes for a split second.

"I'm sorry, I don't mean to stress you out. I was curious but I overstepped."

"No, it's okay. I do have to think about these things. Ambrose has said he'll always see me the same way. I guess, as a reaper, he can see past physical appearance."

"Right, sure . . ." Seth says.

"I do want kids someday, but I haven't brought the issue up with him. If we can't have a baby, we could adopt."

"What if you do get pregnant, and the baby is part reaper? Where would it live?"

I swallow hard and run my fingers through my hair. Can that happen? What would I do with a half-reaper baby? That's probably impossible anyway. As Seth says, Ambrose is . . . undead.

"Are you okay? Do you want to stop and rest?"

"No, no it's okay. I'm fine. Let's keep going." An awkward silence hangs between us. "You know, we um—" I clear my throat. "Ambrose and I still haven't . . . " I don't even know why I'm telling him this. I guess him being here and knowing he likes me and is jealous of Ambrose and us being together makes me want to ease some of the tension away from visitation.

"You've never what?"

"We've never been together before. Sexually," I finish, my cheeks burning hot.

Seth nods through the dim lighting. "I see . . . Saving it for marriage or something?"

A low chuckle escapes my throat. "No, nothing like that. We've just been taking it slow, I guess. He's new to all this, you know, the human experience." I part my hands in front of me.

"I get it, but you know, there's no time like when you think you might never see each other again."

"Oh." I laugh. "I don't know. I'm sure it'll be very emotional when I see him. I hardly think there'll be time for any of that. Besides, I want it to be special when we do get there . . ."

Seth slants his smile and shrugs.

"Seth?"

"Yeah?"

"Thank you. For coming out here with me. For worrying about me."

Seth's eyes light up. "You don't have to thank me, Addie. That's what friends are for."

The symbols become scarce as Deacon continues to lead the way. Pretty soon we're back walking through pitch-black corridors, unable to see the path ahead of us.

"You're going to want to stay close to me along these parts." Deacon raises her voice and it echoes in the vastness. Seth and I speed up a little. My eyes struggle to adjust to the darkness. It takes me a few moments to see the dark hooded figure floating in the air. It turns slowly toward us and when I think it will reveal a face, its opened hood reveals a black hole. Even though I can't see any eyes, nor lips, or any features of any kind, I can still feel it staring in our direction. I inch closer to Seth and Deacon as the figure glides straight at us. Seth grabs for my hand but I don't pull away.

Deacon whispers to us as the figure glides closer to me. "Do not move a muscle."

Chills chase up my spine and I press myself closer to Seth. Whatever this thing is, it is emanating intense fear and loneliness. My heart sinks. Glimpses of my brother's death emerge from my memory. The sudden realization I would never see him again and the possibility I may never get back to my father catches in my throat. A vision of my father sobbing into his hands by himself makes my heart skip a beat. Seth pulls me closer as if he knows what I'm feeling. "What is this thing?" I ask.

"Shh . . . don't move."

It gets close enough that I can feel a cold, magnetic pull coming from inside the hood. I try to block out the memories, but it's too late. They're fixed in my mind. I hold my breath and squeeze Seth's hand.

It finally backs away and glides off into the darkness. I let out my breath. "What the hell was that?"

"A revitalizer." Deacon says. "This won't be the only one either."

"A what?"

"Revitalizer. They clear the planes of unnatural thought. Kind of like vacuum cleaners, or how a catfish cleans the ocean reef."

"Unnatural thought? What the hell did it want with me?"

"It sensed that you're human. Humans constantly deal with internal conflicts."

"So, why was it only interested in me? Why not Seth?"

"Maybe you have more baggage than I do."

I don't need to look at Seth to know he's smiling at me. I scoff.

"That was only one of them. If there were more, you both would have been in trouble. The only way you're going to make it out of here, Addison, is to gather your strength. You have to meditate and calm your mind to perform magickal acts. Concentrate on something still, or pure."

"How about just a happy thought?" Seth offers.

"No. Not good enough here. A happy thought can bring other kinds of emotions. Positive and negative thoughts are more complicated than you think. These creatures aren't evil beings. They'll be interested in happy memories as well."

Seth's hand tightens around mine. I stifle a gasp and let go. "How come only sad memories surfaced then?" I ask.

He places his hand on my arm and gently tugs me forward. "How 'bout we both think of the moon?"

Fearful there might be more revitalizers ahead, I take one slow step in front of the other. The air is still warm and dry, and my mouth is dry from thirst. My stomach grumbles. Shit, I hadn't thought about food or water when I decided to jump through a portal in such a hurry.

We walk until Deacon and Seth come to an abrupt stop, causing me to bump into him. Seth moves in front of me, shielding me from whatever is causing us to stop. I gulp.

Looking over his shoulders, there are dozens of black hooded figures.

"Holy . . . shit." I let out a gasp. "Deacon, can't you just fight these guys off?"

"Not really, no."

"Can't or won't?"

Deacon shoots me a look. "Just do what I told you, and they'll move on."

"Don't worry Addie, it'll be easy. Focus on the moon with me, remember?"

His attempts to calm me down are starting to get on my nerves. "How are you so calm? You have never meditated a day in your life."

Seth picks my hand up again and squeezes. "Shhhh. Come on, Addison, close your eyes and try."

I close my eyes and picture the moon. *Don't worry Addie.* What an idiot. Okay, forget him. Concentrate. The moon, the moon. A clear image of a full moon glowing brightly in a starlit sky appears in my mind. I steady my breathing, deep and regular, just like how I begin a spell. Keep thinking about the moon. A memory swoops in. I'm lying on a towel at the beach with my ex-boyfriend, Carl, by my side. Fury forms in the pit of my stomach. He had never been real, a smoke screen to keep me from figuring out that my patient was really my father. And then an image of Ambrose killing Carl with his scythe cuts through. The wave of emotions that come after floods my thoughts, and then my heart warms. Ambrose had saved me, and he played a part in saving Dax. I miss him so much.

Oh no. No, no, no. Think of the moon Addison.

I keep my eyes closed tightly and picture the moon again, afraid if I open them, I will feel defeat and ruin everything. No matter what, the end game is to find Ambrose. Focus on the moon. I open one eye and my fears are confirmed. A revitalizer stands right in front of me, its hood opened, like a vacuum in space. More of them advance behind that one. I twist my neck from side to side and my stomach knots. They're coming in from all directions. What else can I think of? The ocean? No, same problem. Think Addison, think. Something else that's pure.

The air grows cold again. "Deacon? Seth?" I can't hear them anymore. My gut feels empty. Maybe Seth's meditation didn't work for him either. Oh no! What could they be doing to him? I inch to the side, trying to get past them but the more I move, the faster they approach. More and more of them, surrounding me. Deacon failed to tell me what would actually happen if they did catch me. I can't help but picture the worst. My and Seth's souls being sucked out of existence. Just vacuums doing their jobs, cleaning the filth from the astral corridors. Like none of us ever mattered.

This isn't helping.

I stand on the tips of my toes to see if I can catch a glimpse of Deacon or Seth, but the hooded figures stretch taller, blocking my view. Thoughts fly into my mind at such a speed I can't focus. All that time practicing meditation and magick completely thrown out the window. Wait, there's magick. Deacon didn't say *I* can't try magick. I concentrate my will on forming a ball of energy. The palms of my skin are like ice. I rub them together and concentrate. The figures maintain their focus on me. I visualize a ball of beautiful white light forming in the center of my hand. I move my hands in and out to form a magnetic field. But after a few tries, nothing emerges. I would be able to do this at home with my eyes shut. What if I summon a sword? I visualize my dagger and its ruby hilt and how badly I wish I had it with me.

The figures begin to move closer. One of them closes in on my face, and my knees grow weak with fear. I lower myself onto the floor. My face is frozen, and I can't blink. Sadness overpowers me as my insides tear apart, into the depths of time and space.

REAPER IN THE RAINFOREST

DAX

Something wet and slimy runs down my cheek. I slap my face to wipe it away and open my eyes to the bright sunlight. Chattering comes from a hairy creature hanging upside down over me, with round, brown eyes and saliva falling from its mouth. Aw, gross! I jump up and spin around. It's a brown, furry monkey, now grinning widely at me. I wipe more off my face. Disgusting. It dashes over to a little girl with red paint coating her hands. She stumbles back, screams, and hits her knees on a tree root. She fumbles to her feet only to fall on her bottom. Water wells up in her eyes as they meet mine and she starts to cry. The monkey screeches and bolts up a tree.

Where the hell am I? Tall trees with enormous philodendron leaves climbing their trunks surface the area. The air is thick and moist. If I wasn't already dead, I would probably be itching and burning beneath my black cloak. How the fuck did I get here? I reach for my scythe inside my cloak. *Shit.* I run my hands all along my cloak and my trousers. Nothing. It's gone. I pinch the top of my nose and

"

close my eyes. Okay, don't panic. What's the last thing I remember?

Oh fuck. Ambrose. I remember someone stabbing Ambrose and tossing him into a portal. But there's no way to actually kill a reaper, is there? I rub my head. So, either someone stole my scythe, too, or it fell somewhere when I landed. Shit, I can't think. I dart my eyes at the toddler, who is still wailing her eyes out. What is this place?

Careful not to startle her even more, I slowly inch toward the little girl and squat down beside her.

"It's okay, I won't hurt you." The little girl sniffles and wipes her face, spreading the red paint from her hands onto her cheeks. "Where are your parents?" She looks up at me and puts her dirty fingers in her mouth. The monkey swings from the tree and lands on my back.

The little girl laughs and points at her pet. "Digo!"

"Digo?" I turn to face the monkey on my shoulder. "Is your name Digo?" The monkey looks at me and grabs my nose hard before he jumps off and circles around me. "Ouch! You little shit!"

Leaves rustle behind me and I jump to my feet. Voices and footsteps come from behind some shrubs and trees. "Could that be your parents looking for you?" Twigs crunch beneath me as I take a few steps closer to get a better look. As I push the dense undergrowth aside, a sharp arrow darts through the forest and pierces my chest.

I wrap my hand around the arrow and pull it out of my chest in one blow. I drop the arrow and my coat on the ground. If being all dressed in black in the middle of the rainforest doesn't scream outsider, add a reaper suit.

A handful of men and boys wearing red tribal paint inch out from the trees with sharp spears and arrows. Some of them stare open-mouthed at the sight of me pulling an arrow out like it was nothing. One of the young boys moves in closer, pointing his bow and arrow right at my face. I glance down at him and can't help smiling. "It's okay, you can put that down."

"*No te muevas*. Don't move," one of the men tells me.

I hold my hands out so they can see them. "I'm not going to hurt any of you."

"*Es un muerto!*"

The little girl comes walking in with her monkey as if she doesn't have a care in the world, as if several of her tribespeople are not pointing sharp weapons at a stranger. "Daddy," she calls, and goes running to a man with red tribal paint over his eyes. The monkey jumps back on my shoulder.

I turn to the man who called me a walking dead man in Spanish. I recognize their Peruvian accent and immediately know where I am. "Easy now, I'm actually *undead*." Like that will ease their worries. I take a step forward and the man in front nudges his spear toward me. He wears a band around his head and his paint covers the entire right side of his face. One of the men says something in a different language, and if I hadn't been a reaper, I never would have understood what came next.

The little boy puts his bow and arrow down. There's low murmuring and chatter. I can hear them whispering about me being sent from the underworld to destroy their village.

"I am not here to cause any harm," I say to them in Spanish. I'm not even sure why I'm here, for that matter. The little girl's father speaks up.

"A monkey would not come close to an undead man that would bring harm to our people."

I glimpse at Digo who is still on my shoulder, busy eating something in his hands and stops to look up, as if put in the spotlight. He jumps off and goes back to the little girl.

"I promise I bring you no harm." I hold my arms up in a gesture of peace.

The girl's father speaks again. "Why are you here?"

"I—" I flick my eyes back and forth. I don't actually have an answer.

Unconvinced, the man moves forward and presses his spear against my shoulder, pushing me to walk.

"Come with us, move."

Leaving my cloak behind, I walk with them about a quarter of a mile to a less shaded village filled with straw huts and several fire pits dotting the ground. An acrid, smoky smell assaults my nostrils. I look over to a small group of women around a big pot cooking something purple that smells like sweet potato. One of the young ladies chews on something, then opens her mouth and spits out a long glob of purple spittle into the pot. I grimace. Good thing I'm not hungry.

"Keep moving," one of them says as he presses his spear to my back. What part of *their spears cannot hurt me* do they not understand? I bite down my annoyance, wanting to avoid any further conflict with them. Keep cool, Dax, keep a clear head. It's best to remain respectful. At least it will buy me time to think. They shove me to a grassless patch in the center of their community. *So the whole village can keep an eye on me.*

"We will consult with the shaman; you must stay here."

Several locals walk up to me slowly, curious and afraid of the talk that I'm sure is spreading fast. Small village and all that. I can only imagine what they're saying. A desolate village in the middle of the Peruvian rainforest. I've heard of these people before. They're indigenous and prefer life away from modern civilization.

I don't know how far their shamanic wisdom goes, or if they even have reapers in their belief system. Either way, it is probably best to keep this as a fast visit. I need to get back to the astral plane. Or home to my sister.

The little boy who had aimed a bow and arrow at my face approaches, still holding his weapon and followed closely by Digo. I greet him with a smile and stick my hands up in the air again. A half smile spreads on the kid's face and he lowers his bow.

I crouch down and Digo jumps onto my shoulder. The little boy takes out a small piece of banana and motions for me to give it to his furry friend. Digo takes the piece of banana and sticks it in his mouth. I laugh and the boy grabs my hand, placing his on top of my palm. His eyes widen and he grins widely as he compares the size of his little hand to mine. A few other kids see the interaction and run over. A taller boy, maybe a year or two older, wearing a bright orange top, grabs onto my arm, pressing into my bicep. The kids exchange laughs and I can't help but laugh too.

"Don't worry, one day you'll grow big and strong too."

The boy with the arrow takes me by the hand and pulls me to a small hut with an open straw door. A lady runs toward us, waving her arms at the boy.

"*Mijo, venga para qui!* Come here, this man is not safe." She runs over and pulls her son away, while wrestling the little girl I saw earlier in her arms. I turn to face the woman and hold my hands out in front of me. I tell her in Spanish that I'm not here to harm anyone, that I'm just lost. She continues to pull her son away, although her face softens. That's something at least.

Digo stays put. "Like being on my shoulder, little monkey?" It's probably Digo's trust in me that calms her down. She lets her son go, and he runs toward an elderly woman walking out of the hut. The woman holds a hot pot in her hands and walks toward us. She gives me a crooked grin as she sets the pot down on a wooden table. "*Venga.*" She beckons for everyone to gather around the stew.

"I don't think he eats, mama."

"Well, that's okay if he doesn't. He will still join us for supper."

A smile creeps up on my face at her willingness to be hospitable toward me while everyone else has their guard up. She appears to be the eldest, the wise one, maybe not the rule maker, but she might as well be.

I take my seat on an empty bench and the little boy sits down next to me.

"We have not met properly. My name is Palla and I know who you are."

I raise an eyebrow. Does she really?

"We have been talking. Many here think you are a *muerto*, but we, the oldest ones in the forest, recognized the black hood. We do not have your kind in our stories, but I have been to other places. Is it I you have come for? Or someone else?"

"I haven't come for anyone."

Palla scrunches up the wrinkles on her forehead. "Then what by God's name are you doing out here with the Ashaninka?"

What can I say? That there was a fight with a demon, and I got banished to the rainforest? None of it would make any sense.

More and more tribe people gather around with plates, some carrying pots of food.

"I'm not at liberty to discuss how I got here, but I can tell you that I'm not supposed to be here and need to get back home."

Palla takes one long look at me, one eye wider than the other. She's suspicious. Hell, I would be too if I were a tribal man in the rainforest and the freaking grim reaper appeared out of nowhere. I can only imagine how this must look.

"Is there a way I can borrow a phone to make an international call?"

"In town, yes. But someone will have to take you there tomorrow. It is too late now. Why does the Grim Reaper need to use a telephone?"

"I'm actually just a reaper in training, and there's many of us. The real Grim Reaper hasn't been seen in thousands of years." Everyone grows silent, staring at me.

Now I've done it. "The food smells delicious," is the only thing I can think of that will break the ice.

"Can you eat? I can serve you a plate."

"As of late, I can." Before becoming a reaper, I had been undead and did not crave food and was unable to eat. Since transforming, my physiology has changed in ways that brought back my ability to enjoy certain human activities, like food and coffee, just like Ambrose. Magick is a wonderful thing.

"By the way, I have lost my scythe. Has anyone seen it?"

"Your what?"

"Umm, does anyone have a pencil and paper?"

A young girl, around eleven years old brings out a crayon and a scrap of paper. I thank her and draw a curved blade on the paper and hold it up. "My scythe. I seemed to have lost it when I landed here last night." A few people exchange glances and laugh.

"Not the Grim Reaper, he says." Palla takes the paper and passes it around.

"Well, I am *a* reaper, and we do carry scythes. That much is true."

"We haven't seen it. But we can help you look."

Someone passes me a plate full of purple sweet potato. Oh . . . I definitely don't want that. "That's really kind of you, but no thanks."

She urges the plate at me. "Eat," she says. All eyes are on me. Fuck. In some cultures, it is offensive not to eat what's given to me. Something tells me it's like that here. I take the plate and swallow hard. If Addison could see me now, she would laugh. I take the spoon and bring it up to my lips, opening for a taste. I swish the gloopy mixture around in my mouth for a minute, still hot from the pot. The fresh memory of the girl's spittle surfaces, and I push it back. Despite how it was made, it's actually really delicious.

"I am sorry for how our warriors treated you before. You have to understand that when they recognized you as undead, they had to assume you were coming back from a battle to bring us turmoil. This does happen sometimes."

"No need to apologize. They did what was best for everyone, and it could have gone worse. I know this. To be honest, they reacted how anyone would, given the circumstances. They didn't seem too bothered when they saw that I didn't bleed. They just assumed I was dead?"

She smiles. "The ayahuasca teaches us about the spirit." I nod slowly and take another bite. "Tonight, you will meet our shaman."

"Oh? I thought that was you." I say.

She shakes her head and laughs. "No, I am just old."

At night, people circle around a fire inside a large hut. A slender man between five and six feet tall wearing a red headband along with large, beaded necklaces stands talking to Palla. He glances over at me a few times, while I sit with my legs crossed, staring at the flames.

I need to get to a phone. It all seems so surreal—the small talk, the ritual, and how irrelevant it all is. When I was alive, I believed it was pointless to stress about things I couldn't control. But now, despite trying to go with the flow, I'm eager to leave. I have to bide my time and wait for the right moment though. But what if that moment never comes?

The man wearing beads approaches me. "I want to welcome you to our ceremony on this night. I am the shaman."

"It's a pleasure to meet you." I stand up and take the shaman's hand. He has a soft face and looks young, but his eyes say differently. "I doubt your . . . hallucinogen would really have any effect on me."

The shaman tilts his head to the side, the dim light of the fire accentuating his pointy chin and high cheekbones. "For us, it is an honor that you are visiting. At first, we had to be wary because we believe if someone dead comes back to us, it is someone from battle seeking revenge. But I see that this is not the case. So now, it has come to my attention that you being here with us is no accident."

It is *definitely* an accident.

"It is my belief that you have been brought to us on this night for a reason. Palla tells me that you lost something of yours?"

"Ah, yes. My scythe. I use it to . . . well, er, among other things, I need it to go back home." The shaman leans back a bit and nods.

"During this ceremony, some will be taking ayahuasca.

This is an ancient plant of the rainforest. When taken, the plant gives us the ability to attain universal knowledge. For hundreds of years, it has taught us how to heal and has taught us wisdom. We will use it tonight to help you find what you are missing. But you will not drink."

I lower my gaze at him. "Why do you think I'm here?"

"For many years, my people have been under threat. But most importantly, the rainforest has been under threat. You see, the Ashaninka people, we have one goal, and that is to protect and save the rainforest. Be here tonight, standing watch while we commence our spiritual journey. It may last for several hours. I will be guiding them, so I too will keep watch and protect them. Ayahuasca is the way of my people. It is important to do these rituals. If you can be here and help to keep us from harm . . ."

"Say no more. I will stand guard during your ritual." I lend him a warm smile, which is reciprocated. I don't know how much outside experience the shaman has but he seems to be comfortable with my presence. It seems only right to offer to help, especially if it could help find my scythe.

I sit back against the wall while a group of ten take their concoction from the shaman and sit down. Palla stands up with a smoking bundle of sage. She walks from person to person, wafting the smoke over their bodies. I watch as they drink, their faces growing weary before they vomit and lay down. The shaman explains to me that this is normal, the ayahuasca cleans you out first before you ascend. He brings out some of the vine for me to see, pleased about getting to share some of his knowledge with me. I take it from him and bring it closer to the light.

My body lands with a loud thud. The last thing I remember are the dancing flames from the fire and holding the vine in my hand. I open my eyes to find myself surrounded by complete darkness, accompanied by the drip, drip, drip sound of water nearby.

I know that sound.

I stand up and wait until my eyes adjust to the low light. I look down and see that I still don't have my cloak. Okay, that means I wasn't dreaming. How the hell did I get back? I start to walk down the cold corridors, passing a few images of demons etched into the stone, to find my way back to my own quarters, when a cry for help bounces off the walls.

"Seth! Deacon? Where are you? Help!"

Recognizing the voice, I bolt. "Addison? Addison! What the hell are you doing here?" I run, water pushed by my feet. Then I see her. Backed up into a corner, surrounded by revitalizers.

I need to do something quick. But what without my scythe? I move forward, getting between my sister and the revitalizer. I stand right in front of her, but Addison can't see me. I rush toward the revitalizer, but it disappears into gray smoke.

What the hell?

I crane my neck back to Addison, but she's no longer there. In fact, I'm no longer standing in the corridors. I turn around to see three bars in a tiny window. I'm in a cell. Sigils are carved into the walls. I follow them around the room, trying to decipher their meaning. That's when I see the figure in the corner. I'd recognize that red hair poking out from beneath her cloak anywhere.

I squat down and lift her chin. "Deacon? Can you hear me?" Her skull bobs back down but she doesn't reply. "Deacon?" I try again, raising my voice. The smell of something burning fills my nostrils. With each blink, my vision morphs and changes. Visions of the hut from the rainforest come into view.

I open my eyes again, wincing at the smoke. I'm back at the ceremony. Touching the ayahuasca must have induced me. Was it real, or was it only a vision? Screams from men and women jolt me awake. I shoot up as pieces from the roof slam down in front of me. The hut is on fire! People dash for the opening, screaming in fear.

"You must get up," the shaman says to me. "We are under attack."

"DARK AS A DUNGEON"

ADDISON

I blink myself awake as my name bounces off the stone walls of these hollow chambers. My head is heavy as I try to lift it off the cold damp floor, but I almost want to remain asleep.

"Addison!" a familiar voice calls again.

The frost stings my face as I regain consciousness. "Ambrose?" I nudge myself up by my elbow, squinting through the darkness. Where am I?

Footsteps splash toward me and the soft lighting coming from the top of the pillars outline a moving image as I flick my eyes upward.

"Addison, are you hurt? I've been so worried!"

Are my eyes deceiving me? His chestnut hair lays wet and flat against his forehead as he reaches down to lift me up. "Ambrose?"

"Yes, it's me, Addie. I missed you so much."

I part my lips, ignoring the fact that they're trembling from the biting cold. "I can't believe it's really you . . ." I take his arm as he helps me. Butterflies swarm in my stomach as his eyes pierce into me. Oh, how I missed those ocean blue eyes! "Oh my god, Ambrose . . . it's really you." I grab his face and press my lips against his cold, soft mouth. His hands wrap around my waist, bringing me in, and my leg wraps around his. His tongue licks my teeth as he backs up, with me moving with him, until his back is flat against the wall.

My hands wander up his chest and an electric tingling courses between my legs. I've never wanted anyone so badly in my life but now is not the time. I gently pull away. Kissing him one more time, I let out a soft giggle. "My god, I missed you." Our foreheads meet and we exhale in unison. A wide grin appears on both of our faces as I take a short step back.

"I missed you too," he says. "I wasn't sure I'd ever see you again."

"Me neither." I touch the side of his face with my palm and he closes his eyes, leaning into it. "How did I get here?" I say, flicking my eyes around and stopping at a tiny hole on a wall with bars on it.

"A revitalizer appeared and dropped you here. But Addison . . . there's no way out."

"Have you been in this cell this whole time?" I look back into his eyes, but they seem drawn back. Somehow more distant than usual. Almost like it really isn't him. But of course it is. He must have already gone through so much. "How long have you been here?"

"I've lost count. Time passes differently here anyway." His voice is dry and even. My heart sinks to the pit of my stomach. I have got to get him out of here. I understand what happened now. Azazel used the revitalizer to bring me here to hold up his end of the deal. The only question is, how am I going to get back to Seth and Deacon? Will they be looking for me?

"Ambrose . . . I have to get you out of here. Do you know anything about how the cells down here work?"

He nods. "They're guarded by Enochian sigils." I dart my eyes around looking for them, but I don't see anything carved on the walls. In fact, I don't even see those grotesque demons doing unspeakable things to one another. That's one thing I'm glad about not being here.

"They're probably hidden or on the outside of this cell though. Azazel was clever enough to know how to keep me out, it seems."

I sigh. "Shit, how are we going to do this?"

"To be honest Addison, I'm just happy to see you." He brings me in closer and plants another kiss on my lips. I kiss him back, smile, and inch away. We need to come up with a plan.

"I am too, but we need to go. I don't know how long Azazel is going to let me be in here with you."

Ambrose raises a brow. "How exactly did you persuade him to let you stay in here with me, Addison?"

My cheeks burn and I raise my brows. "I . . . sorta made a deal with him."

Now his brows are arched to his forehead. "What kind of deal? Addison . . ."

"He wants me to open the cage that has his father. But don't worry, I don't plan to. Which is why we need to figure out a way to get you out of here, so we can go."

"Go where? Azazel has this whole place rigged."

He's right. And without Deacon's scythe or his, we can't open a portal. Even if we could, Azazel would follow us there anyway. "Deacon said something about getting to the Akashic level so that we could use the water to find answers."

"Deacon is here?" His eyes light up. "Good. I was afraid she would have been captured too."

I nod once, fighting back the tears forming at the corners of my eyes. I still don't know anything about my brother. "I don't know where Dax is though."

"If Deacon is with you, you should be able to make it to the Akashic level. Once there, she'll know where to go. Honestly Addison, I don't know why you came. This place is dangerous for a human. Deacon could have done this on her own."

I stifle a laugh and swallow. "What can I say? I'm hard-headed. And . . . you would have done it for me." I take his hand. "Hey, do you know anything about me having to prove myself? I keep hearing that I'll have to prove myself to the Akashic plane."

"The Akashic is the purest form of water so your spirit needs to be from here, and not human," he says, tilting his head to the side. "The planes run on raw energy; you're going to have to learn how to use your magick there. You'll be fine."

I screw up my features. Not human but learn to use my magick here. An image of me trying to summon my powers right before the revitalizer got me surfaces in my memory. "Can I not use my powers here?"

He shakes his head. "Afraid not, Addie. The closer you are to the prisons, the more your powers are dampened. But the closer you are to the mental plane; the more you can use them again. Unfortunately, you'll pass the mental plane by the time you get to the Akashic. Only reapers have power there."

"Azazel said something about me being the only one who could use the dagger to open the cage though . . . Why would that be if I can't even use my powers?"

Ambrose's eyes soften as he lends me a bleak smile. "Only he knows, I guess. Do what he says. You might just become strong enough to get me out." His eyes move past me and fall toward the corner of the cell. I crane my neck back to see what he's looking at.

A dark patch emerges, growing in size. I let out a short gasp.

"Looks like it's time for you to go."

"No, I don't want to leave you." I wrap my arms around his neck and pull into him, kissing him gently.

"I don't think you have a choice."

"I will come back for you, I promise." I swallow hard as he kisses me one more time, taking my breath away. I hope I get to see him again. I shake that out of my head. Of course I will. I have to.

My eyes force themselves closed as emptiness and sorrow fill my soul. The last thing I see is his fingers leaving mine as I get swallowed into the seemingly endless void of the revitalizer.

⋈

Seth's face comes into focus. I blink my eyes open and catch his gaze as he strokes my hair with his fingers. I edge myself up to my elbows.

"Easy there, Addison."

I gasp, arching myself up. "Where's Ambrose?"

"Ambrose? Umm . . ." Seth lets out a chuckle . . . "Deacon? A little help?"

I nudge myself up. Why the hell did I have my head on Seth's lap? "What the hell happened?" I shout.

"You fainted. What do you remember? One second you were on the floor and that thing was over you, and the next thing I knew you were gone. Then I turned back around and there you were again!"

"Time works differently here," Deacon says. "Addison, you went somewhere, didn't you?"

I pinch the top of my nose. "Yeah, I saw Ambrose. I was in the cell Azazel is keeping him in."

"And? What did he say?"

"Nothing we don't already know." I dust myself off as I stand and lean against the wall. One of the demons in the images turns to show me his bottom. I grimace and push myself off. "Nice." Stupid things. "He only said that your plan of going to the Akashic level is the only sensible plan we got. He didn't offer anything useful. In fact, he just sounded lonely, and distant . . ." My stomach churns. "And nothing about my brother."

"Don't worry Addison, we'll find him too," Seth says, putting a hand on my shoulder. I smile and nod at him.

"Well, leave it to Ambrose to offer useless information. Come along then, let's get moving," Deacon spits. I force down my urge to retort. Whatever annoying relationship they have is just fluff. I know Deacon obviously cares about him. Otherwise, she wouldn't be doing this.

"Where to now?" I say.

"Next up, the mental plane."

HELD CAPTIVE

DEACON

"Deacon."

My nose twitches as a man's voice echoes in my ears. *Dax?*

"Deacon!"

I jolt awake.

Sigils radiate a fiery glow inside a dark, cramped area, forcing my eyes to come into focus from the surrounding darkness. "What the?" I scramble to get up but groan as I strain against the heavy chains pulling me apart. "What is this?" I say, jerking my arms down. "Where am I?" I yank down on the chains, repeatedly, trying to free myself. Looking closer, there are sigils embedded into the cuffs.

Captivus.

How the hell did I get here and who would go so far as to imprison a reaper? What could *I* have done? Hundreds of sigils illuminate the cell walls as I gloss over them. Someone went through a lot of trouble to keep me imprisoned.

Wait . . . Does that mean . . .? I listen closely for the thoughts of any other reaper who could be nearby.

Blocked.

That's curious. One of these sigils must be muffling my telepathy.

The brassy sound of metal scraping against the stone floor passes outside the door. That'll undoubtedly be a guardsman with his ax. I'll have to get past that guy too if I can find a way through these sigils and out of these cuffs. I give it another pointless yank. The sound of the ax on stone fades away. There aren't any prison guards with the ability to talk I can call out to, and it's not like we can make phone calls. Only entities designed to keep the corridors clean. Sigils are enough to keep prisoners in. I'm completely screwed.

How long until someone from the High Council notices I'm gone and comes looking for me? What if they already know I'm here? No, no . . . That could only mean they put me in here themselves. I think I would know if I had done something wrong. I gasp. They found out about Ambrose and Addison and they know that I was keeping it a secret. That has to be it. Why else would I be chained up? Does that mean Ambrose is . . . is . . . gone forever? I pull on the chains again, causing them to clank against the walls.

If somebody does come by, it will be to give me a trial date. If no one comes by, then I'm a prisoner for eternity. Either way, I could be in here for centuries.

But I cannot let that happen. I don't deserve this, do I? What's the last thing that happened? I nudge on the chains a bit harder, trying to prop myself up from sliding. Dax's voice. His voice woke me up, but where the hell is he?

The screeching of the ax against the stone floor makes another round. The big lurch of a figure moves outside through the tiny window.

An idea sparks in my brain. They might respond to a reaper. It's worth a shot.

"Hey, buffoon! I command you to enter this cell." I wait a few moments, but it continues to walk away. There has to be something missing, like part of my memory of how I ended up here. I study the sigils on the ground. One is shaped like a tilted diamond with a sword piercing through it. This must be a holding sigil. Meant to keep me in. My powers will be dampened, no doubt. But maybe I can rig it.

I'll have to resort to sorcery though. I hate magick. Tilting my head, I look back up at my chains. I don't think I have another choice. Son of a bitch, here goes nothing.

I concentrate on my memories. All reapers have the ability to access the Akashic waters, enabling us to gain vast knowledge. I have been gifted with telepathy from reaper to reaper. I can speak to other reapers through my mind and can sometimes tell the consequences of what's going to happen, but this isn't always accurate. But this power is of no use now. However, if I can reach into my Akashic memories, maybe I can find out how to break these sigils.

I picture myself standing before the deep blue waters. I can almost hear the flowing streams, and then my memories take over.

Now, think back to the time I saw this symbol. I picture the diamond-shaped sigil flowing in the waters, the ripples moving rhythmically. The waters on the surface grow darker as I scry.

The unsettling sound of the guardsman shakes my concentration. I open my eyes to the dull cell walls. Shit. Let's try that again.

I slow my breathing. *Access my memories.* The sigil emerges in the dark waters as before. A scythe imprinted on a shield appears first. Then a large dagger draws itself over the shield and blocks the scythe. The symbols glow as they merge into one sigil. That's it. So how do I break it?

The ripples distort the sigil, allowing for a new image to take shape, a sideways *V* facing the left, with another *V* facing it, looking toward the right. They move in on each other, and a skull emerges from the depths and fuses with the rune.

That was it? A rune and a skull? Was that a riddle? How do I cast it if I can't inscribe it?

Opening my eyes again, I focus on my cuffs and the sigils and visualize the binding rune. I concentrate hard, imagining the skull fusing with the rune and releasing it.

I yank on my chains, but nothing happens. Still strapped in. What the hell? I *really* hate magick! I'm not practiced at this shit. The chains hit the wall behind me as I let myself drop, sounding like a sack of bones hitting the floor. I stare out to the sigils on the floor and let out a deep, heavy breath. One of the warding sigils sweeps away like dust.

I lift a brow. How did that happen?

I visualize the binding rune in my head again and focus my energy on my chains. A few moments later, I try to wriggle free, but as before, I'm bound by the heavy metal. Letting out a grunt, I pant hard, my chest expanding inside my rib cage. Yet again, another small scripture disappears and the word *captivus* disappears from the right cusp. I pull down hard and the chain breaks free, clattering as it hits the floor.

"Of course. The Judge would chastise me for forgetting the ancient texts so readily . . ." I remember the passages about having to breathe out the runes. That must be how I did it. I look over to my left hand and visualize the rune again, this time breathing it out toward the shackle. The word vanishes and I break loose.

Before attempting to escape, I do the same with the rest of the sigils in the cell. I don't want anything holding me back.

I run toward the door. The sound of metal on stone draws nearer. These beings are meant to locate anomalies within the cells. Could it sense that I banished the sigils and freed myself?

I freeze as it stops right in front of the door. I look through the window and its conical face meets my eye. I take a few steps back as it moves forward, phasing in through the wall.

Oh fuck.

It pulls back his ax. I duck and run into the corner. Guess that answers my question.

The guardsman sniffs the air, turning slowly toward my corner. I could really use my scythe right about now.

It twists its ax again. I inch slowly toward it. "I'm right here."

Twisting its head in confusion, he drops his arm a little, allowing me to kick his inner elbow and take his ax. I hold the weapon in my hands and swing it at his neck, chopping his head off. It hits the stone wall with a thump, leaving his body standing headless in the room. I kick it and watch as it topples over.

No time to celebrate small victories though, I turn around to see I'm still stuck in a locked cell with no way of escape. And there *will* be more guardsmen walking the corridors. I look at the ax, never having seen one up close. If it's similar to a scythe, it might also be a key. I walk with the ax held out in front of me. It merges with the stone as soon as I touch it and I'm able to walk through the wall.

Freed from the restrictions of the cell, my power flows

into my bones. The closer I am to the Akashic level, the stronger I'll be. If only Ambrose could see me now. Normally, he's the rule-breaker and I'm the one keeping him in check. I lean against the wall and take a second to search for him within my mind. Now that I am uncon-strained, it feels good to be able to split my consciousness and search for someone. Careful not to get noticed by the High Council, I quickly scan for Ambrose.

Dread sinks in as I'm met with silence. Could I still be replenishing? I swallow my hopes, as I do feel whole. I try again.

Silence.

I squeeze my eyes and swallow. There was a time I wouldn't have cared if he got incinerated. Times have changed. Behind me, the rattling of an ax being dragged down the corridor thunders in my ears. I stand still, listening to see if I can make out which direction it's coming from. The sound multiplies to many. More are coming. They must have caught wind that something happened. I back up against the wall, sliding myself forward, my robe blending in with the dark stone. The sound grows louder and louder.

A hooded revitalizer makes its way in my direction, ready to consume me. I now know which astral level I'm in. I freeze in place. There is no fighting these creatures, and where there is one, there are many. They must know there's been a breach. They're looking for me.

I inch forward, ignoring the sound of the guardsmen closing in behind me. I catch a glimpse of a small cell window. Another jail cell. Will it keep coming after me if I willingly incarcerate myself? They are gaining on me from both directions; I have no choice. I run out in front of the revitalizer as quickly as I can before it starts sucking me in. There's no telling where it'll take me. I grip onto the ax

I'm still holding and press against the door and walk through it.

On the other side, I find myself in a cell that looks identical to the one I had been in. I move to the window to see if I can see the guardsmen or revitalizer. They're still closing in.

I hold my breath as I stare out. The guardsmen walk past. I let out a sigh of relief as I watch them continue down the corridor. They aren't coming in. The revitalizer, on the other hand, is still there. No doubt more will show up, but at least I know they aren't going to merge through the walls.

It's probably best that I wait in here until it glides away. I turn around and lean against the door. A glint catches my eye and I look up to see sigils covering the walls. Once again trapped, unable to escape without being caught. Shit. Something else catches my eye as I scan the room.

A hooded figure—its face shielded by a cloak; arms chained up to the walls. I move closer. "Ambrose?" I whisper. I crouch, pull the hood, back and gasp. "Judge?"

POCKET SCYTHE

DEACON

"What are you doing here?" I say, although his head hangs down, lifeless. The one person who can sentence me is sitting in a jail cell. "Judge? Can you hear me?" I try propping him up, laying his skull back against the wall, but it rolls over on its side and back down again.

There must be a way to wake him. I scratch my skull. Did Dax really wake me up? His voice seemed to have come out of nowhere. Is he somewhere here, too? But then how did he reach me through all the barriers? Perhaps he went through his memory like I had, but that would mean the prison would have detected a breach long before it had detected me. No, things have been quiet up to this point. Besides, Dax wouldn't know to do that. He hasn't been a reaper long enough. He must be out there somewhere, trying to reach me.

Right, this isn't only about me. If the Judge is here too then . . . I shudder at what this could mean for all of us. What *does* this mean?

I take a confident breath and slap my superior's cheek-bone. "Judge!"

Again, no response. This *can't* be happening.

Getting up, I scan the sigils around the cell, searching for any symbol I might recognize. This time, I need to have a strong plan before breaking any barriers and calling attention to this cell. My bony fingers run over the Enochian signature, in the same place where it had been in my cell. If it's in the same place, then maybe these wards are all in the same place, and the cells are just replicated for reapers, not taking into consideration that some of us might be stronger than others. If this is true, we could get out of here. A heavy chain moves behind me. I turn to see the Judge waking up and I fall to my knees at his side. He lets out a grunt, narrows his eyes at his constraints, and grimaces.

"Judge? You're awake."

"Deacon?" He pulls on his chains and leers at me, his frown deepening. "What is the meaning of this?"

"I don't know. I woke up the same way you did. We're prisoners."

"Prisoners? How?"

I take a seat in front of him. "Judge, what is the last thing you remember?"

He stares down at his robe. "Well, I . . . I can't recall," he says as his voice becomes raspy with each word. "What is happening? Where is my scythe?"

"I woke up without my scythe too." I open my hands and robe to show him that I have nothing. "It appears something terrible has happened. Our memories have been wiped, and we were stripped of our scythes and imprisoned."

I relax my shoulders as his demeanor becomes less accusatory, but he searches my eyes for truth in my words.

The lines on his forehead wrinkle. "I can't access anything." The terror in his voice is palpable.

"There are sigils all around our cells meant to keep us in. We're as useless as . . . humans," I say, slapping my thighs with the palms of my hands.

The Judge jerks his head back. "How is it that you escaped? Unleash me."

"I will, but in a moment. You might want to try something first. The restraints are protected by high magick. I sourced my memories from the Akashic waters, or at least *my* memories of them. I still have my long-term memory. I found out how to break the sigil that keeps us here. Then I made a run for it."

His eyes fall down at the ax by my side. "You've always been the resourceful one. Right then, allow me."

"Wait. There's something else. We're imprisoned in one of the lower levels. We're in LLAPS, meaning that the—"

"Guards will vanquish us if we're found."

I gulp. They can't kill us, but vanquishing us sounds worse than being dead. I imagine it would be like . . . being alive but split into pieces across the ether. "Yes, that's how I found your cell. I was escaping a revitalizer." I inch closer, dropping my voice down to a whisper. "Judge? Do you know who could have done this, and why?"

He shakes his head. "No, but I suppose we'll find out. Nothing is ever erased in the Akashic level, just suppressed."

"Well, look at this sigil here," I say, pointing to the same emblem I scried earlier. "It looks demonic, but different from all the rest of their scriptures. Older. And this symbol here." I point down to one of the symbols crossing the overall sigil. "I haven't seen anything like it before. It must be before my time as a reaper."

The Judge widens his eyes but stays silent.

"The moment I release you, guards will come. Do you think you can find out who this is before we make an escape? I couldn't find out, but I think that once we know, we'll know what we're dealing with." I look at the Judge pleadingly, knowing he's uncomfortable with his arms chained up, but the more knowledge we have, the better the chances we have of surviving our escape.

"I'll give it a try."

While I wait for the Judge to access his memories, I study other sigils around the room. Nothing else pops out at me. One of them could be the sigil created to craft the prison. Dismantling it could set us free, but it'll most likely let out everyone or everything else at this prison.

The guardsmen make their rounds again. I hold my breath and wait for them to pass, listening to see if they would notice the number of prisoners in the cells had changed. As they pass our cell, a loud crack goes off behind me. I swish my neck back to see that the Judge has pulled free. "No, this is *not* the plan!"

The cuffs around his wrist disappear as he stands up.

"There's a multitude of guardsmen outside. They're going to come in," I whisper.

"Let them come."

I stare at him in disbelief. "But we're defenseless."

The Judge extends his arm and summons his scythe to fit in his hand. I part my lips. "Being a Judge has its advantages. I had a spare."

"How did you get your powers back?" I gape.

"I know who is behind all this. The entire council is—"

He's interrupted by a smashing sound outside the door.

"Is what?"

"Later, now take my hand."

I grab hold of the Judge's bony fingers, wincing at what is about to happen. The Judge is the only one who can teleport, and it isn't something I'm fond of. But I suppose using a portal would call out an alarm. His scythe glows a bright blue light and we teleport out of the prison.

The courtroom is ransacked. I let go of the Judge, steadying my balance, and cup my hands over my mouth. The Judge bends down to pick up a torn up robe.

I turn to face my superior. "What happened here? What did you see in your memories?"

"You were here as well, Deacon. And you fought admirably. But there was nothing you could do. We were outnumbered by our own."

I swallow hard. Our own? Which one of us would do something like this? Then I remember I couldn't reach Ambrose at all. But what motive would he have?

"Someone that I had to lock away a millennium ago, before your time."

I arch a brow, waiting for him to tell me who it is.

"The angel of death, Azazel."

I inhale sharply. "I'm sorry, did you say Azazel? The *demon* Azazel? The one *you* said was locked up and couldn't get out? I would hardly call him one of our own . . ."

The Judge tosses aside the torn fabric. "Long ago, I created the High Council and added order to the system. For hundreds of years, the only chaos we've had has been on Earth. The fallen angels had to be locked up for the safety of the universe."

"So, the rumors have been true all this time. Azazel has escaped." I fall silent for a moment, "Ambrose was right.

Azazel had released Abyzou. He's been planning this for a long time."

The Judge grunts, turning his back to me, and picks up the hilt of a broken scythe.

I resist the urge to roll my eyes at him being dismissive over Ambrose. We all were, and he was right all along.

"The blade is missing. It makes sense now that all the scythes are gone."

I flick my eyes up from the debris at my feet. "Why is that?"

"Azazel is a master of craftsmanship and was a warrior demon with angel blood. He made the blueprints of our scythes and I had them reprogrammed to be unique to each reaper."

"So, where is the rest of the council?"

"Some are torn to pieces in the unknown, I'm afraid. The revitalizers were here. I can sense them. Others are most likely in that prison."

My jaw drops and I snap it back shut. "How did he take our memories? How were you able to access all of yours?" I say, taking a step toward him.

The Judge chafes his jaw line and says, "He's also a very skilled alchemist and has mastered the art of magick. He would be able to tamper with our memories. Taking him down will not be easy." He stares off toward the empty seats of the courthouse, growing silent for a few moments before speaking again. "I recognized his sigil. It wasn't something you would have ever seen or looked for, unlike spells to detain you, I suppose. Those sigils *do* show every reaper. But you wouldn't have known his sigil . . ."

"I thought it looked familiar, but I still couldn't access that memory."

"You most likely had seen it displayed in LLAPS, but you wouldn't have known who it belonged to. You will regain your memory, Deacon, but first we need to get to the Akashic waters."

"I'm ready when you are."

I follow him behind the podium. He moves a black curtain to the side, revealing a door. I follow close behind him through a beige stone corridor that spirals down a steep narrow path.

"This will be the safest path, instead of using the waters in my personal corridor. We still need to be careful. He'll release those minions of his if he catches wind of us lurking about." The Judge slows his pace and turns to face me. "There's something I've been meaning to ask you. How did you wake up on your own? I remember hearing someone call my name and when I woke up, you were there."

"It was Dax," I say. "I heard his voice, but when I opened my eyes, I was alone and chained up."

"This keeps getting curiouser and curiouser."

The sound of the dripping water lets me know we're entering the mouth of the Akashic plane. The area is enormous, but we only need to get to a body of water, it doesn't matter where. The knowledge flows freely here. Anything and everything that has ever happened could be scried within these waters.

"What do you think Azazel wants?"

"He wants to be the angel of death again. To hold dominion over all the planes, including Earth. He never agreed with the order of things, always said that people shouldn't have to face damnation for their sins. Something about them being able to lift themselves up, that they were deserving of more power than they were ever given."

"Well, I don't know anything about sins or what should happen after they die but . . . ." My eyes wander. I never cared to get involved in human affairs. How different are they after they die? Look at Dax. He's at the same level I am now, and he was once alive. Is the human spirit just . . . energy like the rest of us? We all have consciousness after all. Maybe Ambrose was right about caring about them . . .

I shake my head and let out a silent scoff. That's preposterous. Humans can never be like us, with all their feelings and complications.

"Of course, I had to object. He was only ever interested in growing his undead army. He can control the dead, you know . . . I couldn't let him be a dictator. They'd destroy the world. There was an order put in place and I intended to keep it."

"By you?"

"We're here. By me what?" The Judge turns to enter a beige doorway with a high pointed arch.

"Order was put in place by you."

"Oh, well, not all of it. There were things here before me. Anyway, here we are."

A light mist from waterfalls welcomes us as I follow him up the light stone floor to a tall fountain set in front of the Akashic streams. Each entry point has one to avoid contamination.

"Go on Deacon, drink from the water. Get your memories back."

The water here has a fresh smell, like new land that has never been walked on, even though with all the stonework, it clearly has. I take a moment to calm my mind, banishing thoughts of impurities before drinking. When ready, I lower my face and take a sip from the fountain. I lift my head, gasping for air as my memories flood back instantly: the fight, the demonic minions, and the tall demon taking my scythe away.

"I remember." I hang my head over the fountain that is

refilling itself. "Find Ambrose," I direct it. As we stare, images begin to circulate in the water. I wince and ball my fist as images revealing Ambrose in close proximity to Addison sweep past as the records search for his where-abouts. I flick a gaze over at the Judge, searching for disapproval in his face. The images stop at Ambrose being struck in the chest and sent through a portal.

"Enough," the Judge says, and the waters become still.

"Your friend has broken too many laws and it seems he was stripped of his reaping abilities. I think he will stay that way until all this is over."

I stifle a gasp. "He could die," I whisper.

"Then I guess we'll see him again, won't we?" The Judge hovers over the waters. "Find Dax."

Images flood through the waters the same way they did for Ambrose and stop at his current location. "There he is, in a rainforest. He's still a reaper, so we must find him."

"What about his sister? Should she know?"

"Know about what? Her brother's business is ours, not hers. Ambrose is no longer our problem. If he makes it back here, he will be dealt with."

"Right." I don't know if I'm to be prosecuted for keeping secrets, but I'm not about to ask. I've learned my lesson with opening my mouth at the wrong times.

Images in the water start to circulate again. The Judge furrows his brows and I lean in to see what the water is showing us. An image comes into focus. It's Addison. What the hell is she doing here in her physical form? Next to her is a boy I never met. How did he get in? Why would Addison be so reckless?

"What is she doing here?" he spits.

"I don't know. She must have come looking for Ambrose. Wait—who is she with?"

I spread the ripples further to broaden the scene.

They're following someone. But who? As the image comes into focus, I stare at the cloaked figure with red hair. Something down there is pretending to be me.

I ball my fists. That son of a bitch! Addison is here being deceived.

The Judge pulls himself away from the water. "I see why he attacked Ambrose and Dax now."

"Why?"

"Her bloodline was meant to protect a dagger he crafted, long ago. One that would have the power to control all demons, and even rule over us. I had everything secure and he bested me." The Judge slams his fists down.

I stay silent. I've never heard the Judge admit fault before, and the disappointment in his voice makes me uneasy.

"Deacon, I want you to go and retrieve Dax. I have to stay here and help those we left behind in the cells. Right now, there will be complete chaos on Earth. No reapers means extended pain and suffering, no deaths . . ."

"What about—"

"Leave her for now. We have priorities to take care of."

"Right away, your honor. I'll need a scythe."

"Take mine. I'll have enough of my own power to wake everyone up." He reaches into his cloak and pulls out his pocket scythe. "Be careful, this scythe is unique. It can summon every active reaper to you at any moment."

I look at the ax I'm still holding. "Take this as well. It'll help against the guardsmen."

"I was caught unawares before, but now I'll know to use magick," he says, grabbing the ax. He takes out a small bottle from his cloak and fills it with the Akashic water. "A few drops are all I'll need to help the council. I have a feeling war is coming."

CHIMNEY SHAFT

ADDISON

Water reaches my calves as we tread our way through the corridor. At least it isn't as dark as it was when we first started. We can see where we're going. The corridors are a bit brighter but not by much. An orange light comes from the top of the ruins. If there's anything I've learned from the astral plane, differences in atmosphere mean we're in a different location. "We've been walking for hours. Are we getting close?"

Deacon ignores me.

"I thought the mental plane would be drier." Had I known I'd be going caving, I would have worn something different. My hamstrings ache from fighting against the water pressure for so long.

"Hey, at least we're getting a workout," Seth says.

I chuckle. "That's true. How are you doing back there?"

"I'm fine, my mind drifted off for a bit." His voice trails off at the end of the sentence and I pause, craning my neck to wait for him.

"Are you alright?" I say, low enough to keep Deacon

from listening. I know how much she hates human emotions and I don't want to put Seth on the spot in front of her.

"Oh, yeah, I'm great." He forces a smile and I squint one eye.

"Uh huh. Fine, you don't have to tell me. But you came all the way out here for me. I think you can trust me to take a load off," I say.

He runs his hand over his hair, looking to the side. "I trust you Addie," he says in a raspy tone. "I guess I just drifted to issues with my dad, you know? But it's nothing to worry about. Really, I'm fine."

I place a damp hand on his arm. This is the first time I've seen Seth act so serious and contemplative. He's usually always joking with me and making light of every situation, peeving me along the way.

"Honestly Addison, I'm fine," he growls, jerking his arm away slightly. "I guess walking in silence just made my mind drift. I don't really feel like talking about it though, okay?"

I fall behind a bit. "I'm sorry, I wasn't trying to pressure you. I'm just trying to be a good friend . . ." He doesn't answer, so I keep walking.

"Get in front of me," he snaps. "I don't want you falling behind."

"I'm not going to fall behind this time, especially now that I can see where I'm going." Even still, I sludge my way to my spot in between him and Deacon.

I'm silent as we walk the rest of the way, staring down at the water, careful not to trip over anything underneath. My feet grow heavy with each step. I wish I knew how long we had to get to the Akashic level.

Seth clears his throat. "So, uh . . ." My lips pucker. Now he wants to talk?

"How is it going to work between you guys?" Here goes . . . I arch my neck back just a little to see him speeding up behind me.

"How is what going to work?"

"Between you and your boyfriend, I mean." Shit, this again? Can't we just go find him in peace?

"I mean, he's away for *x* amount of time, reaping souls, or whatever, right?"

"Well, erm—"

"And you can't always reach *him*, but he can reach *you* whenever he pleases?"

"Woah, that's not—"

"Doesn't seem like a fair relationship to me." I screw up my face.

"Seth . . ." I sigh. "Our relationship . . . it . . . it's different, that's all. And it doesn't need to be perfect." And I really believe that, I do. I mean, I can't have human expectations when I'm dating a reaper. I'm not an unreasonable person. I'd be setting it up for failure if I did . . .

"If you're sure, Addie. I know that's what you want to believe, but it can't be easy, can it?"

"No, it isn't. But some things are worth the wait. But I guess . . . if we are serious about making this work, I do need to have some sort of expectations, right? Goals? I mean, I'm out here for heaven's sake, in almost-hell, looking for him. That does speak on some level of expectations, doesn't it? So, what's next? Marriage? And then what?" Beads of sweat start rolling down my neck.

"Addison? You okay?"

"Yeah, why?"

"You just got suddenly quiet, is all. I didn't overstep again, did I?" I stifle a scoff. You kinda did, buddy. "I know one thing's for sure, if you were my girl . . ." Okay, now I really need him to stop talking.

"I would never let a doubt about us cross your mind."

"Seth . . . As much as I do agree that things would be easier if I were dating a human, I love Ambrose. I know what you're trying to do. Please just stop." Seth grows quiet. I think that shut him up.

Something orange reflects from the water and catches my eye. It zips past me and I follow it with my gaze.

"What was that?"

"What was what?" Seth says.

"Didn't you see it?

"I didn't see anything."

"Stay close, you two, we're entering the mental plane." Deacon's voice echoes from several feet ahead of us.

I start picking up speed and call out to her. "Hey, Deacon, wait up." But as I lift up a leg, another orange reflection swims out toward me and I jump, splashing water on my shirt. "Ugh, gross!"

"What is it?"

"I don't know, they remind me of those gross silverfish, except longer, and orange." I bend over to take a closer look. The water is becoming murky and I'm glad I don't have anything in my stomach. Another reflection zips through to the opposite direction. And then another in my direction. I still. The fact I know there are nasty looking silverfish in the water makes me wish I could rock climb above it the rest of the way.

"Deacon? Is it safe to walk in this?" I glare at the reflections, Seth next to me, with a disgusted look pasted on his face.

"Let's just go, Addie. I'm sure the quicker we get out of here, the better."

"You're right, I'm just freaked out." Grossed out more than anything. I lift a leg, careful not to step on any of them, when an orange silverfish jumps up at my face. It opens its mouth, showing its piranha-like teeth. I jolt back, falling into Seth, and scream.

He wraps his arm around me, shielding me from the fish as he blocks it back into the water. "What the fuck is that?"

Deacon stops walking up ahead, finally turning and paying attention. "What is going on over there?"

More orange silverfish jump out of the water, their mouths snapping at us with their teeth. Seth grabs me by the hand and pushes me on. We pick up speed, splashing through the water as we reach a deeper area. I'd like very much to not get bit by one of these things.

Deacon's face is grimmer than usual as she stares at me. "When are you going to learn to keep up?"

"Are you kidding?" I spit. "I am keeping up, but there are things . . ."

"In the water. Yes, I know. You're in a different realm, Addison, what did you expect?"

"I think they were trying to eat us."

"Yes, be careful. They eat flesh."

"What the fuck? And you're telling us this *now*?"

"All of this water is contaminated water from the Akashic level. Water that was touched by demons centuries ago, and pushed out to live here. Egregores belonging to demons and prisoners alike lived down here, and became . . . more solid. More lifelike."

My blood curdles. "So, like poltergeists?"

"That is correct. An egregore that lives too long starts to evolve into the emotion it was birthed from, eventually having a mind of its own."

"Are you trying to tell me that the entities we're about to walk into in this place can kill us?"

"Well, some of them, yes. This is the place where nightmares live."

I swallow hard. I thought all egregores were just figments of our darkest emotions: fear, sadness, anger. I knew they would become poltergeists if not dealt with, but I guess I thought that just happened on Earth. But now I see it was foolish to think that.

"Shall we keep going? It'll get drier soon."

"It freaking better. Any deeper and we'll be swimming." I trudge my leg up against the current. The water almost reaches my knees. Contaminated water, filled with evil silverfish. I hate this place. "Yeah, let's hurry up then. The sooner we're out of this disgusting water the better." Something pinches my calf and I jump a foot in the air. "Ow!"

"What happened?" Seth picks up his pace to reach me but then yelps. I gasp and reach down to my leg. A piece of my jeans has been torn up. One of these slimy little bastards bit me!

"Oh shit, Addison!" I snap up to look at him through the dimming light of the corridor as water splashes from him kicking. It takes me a moment before I realize what's happening. Something squirms up my leg and bites me right above my hamstring.

"Holy shit, mother of God!" I reach back and scratch, trying to grab at it through my clothes. Gross! They must be babies or something because they're smaller. Another one bites me a little too close to my crotch for comfort. I have no choice. Pants are coming off. I splash my way to one side of the corridor, trying to find a shallow area through the dark.

"What are you two doing?" Deacon shouts at us from up ahead. "Don't veer off too far. This is a cavernous area. You might drop."

"Drop? Anything else you'd like to share with the class?" I pull my pants down right as one of them shoots up my shirt and bites me under my armpit. Son of a bitch! I reach in and pull out a slimy baby silverfish, biting at the air with sharp teeth. "Yuck!" I fling it back into the water and bites start coming at me furiously. I scream as one bites me under my boob and I fight with my cloak to get my shirt off.

Fuck this clasp! I manage to pull my shirt and my cloak off, but my foot slips, sending me crashing into the murky water. No no no no no! "Deacon! A little help?" I jump up and just as I do, I slip on a loose rock. I take a wobbly step back, lose my footing again, and fall.

But this time when I fall, I slide down an opening.

"Deacon!" Someone grabs my arm. I look down but it's too dark to see how far it goes. I arch my head, expecting to see a reaper, but instead, it's Seth. And he's shirtless. From all my splashing and yelling, I hadn't realized he had to strip down too.

"Hold on Addie, I'll pull you up." I reach up with my other hand and grab onto his arm. I try to feel my way for better footing in the rocks but keep slipping. Great. I'm hanging off a cliff in my bra and panties while my shirtless friend who's crushing on me tries to save my life. Just great.

He lifts me up with incredible strength. Hot damn. As I place my arms around his neck so he can carry me up, a larger silverfish flies at me and slaps me right in the fore-head. I scream, and no thanks to my inability to keep a cool head, I squirm out of his grasp and let go. Seth grabs for me but it's too late. As he reaches, he sticks himself out too far and falls right after me.

"Seth!" my voice croaks. It all happens so fast. I don't know how he does it, but he manages to grab me as we fall. I shut my eyes as he lands on hard slate and a hoarse yell escapes his lungs.

"Are you okay?" he says.

"I think so . . ." Oh my God. My face pales as my bare chest is pressed against his. Where the fuck did my bra go? It must have snapped open while we were falling! No, this cannot be happening. I inch myself up and feel . . . OH MY GOD.

"Seth! Are you . . .?" Naked. Completely, utterly, naked.

NOT AWKWARD AT ALL

ADDISON

"Where are your clothes!?"

He guffaws. "Where are yours?"

"I still have my panties on! My bra just flew off!"

Laughter spits out of his mouth, causing me to bounce up and down on his stomach. I try lifting myself up, covering my breasts with one arm. I hit my elbow hard on the wall. Shit. This is a tight space. "No, I know we had to strip because we were getting bit all over the place. But, you took your underwear off?"

"Oh . . . I uh, wasn't wearing any to begin with and I was getting bit—"

"You don't wear underwear?" So, he just free balls everywhere? Gross! I place my hands on either side of him to try and not . . . touch him, and get a better view of where we fell from, ignoring that as I do, I'm giving him a full-blown view of my breasts. We're going to have to climb our way out of here.

"I find them uncomfortable. We can talk about my wardrobe choices later. What do you say we focus on getting out of here, huh?"

"There's something we both agree on." Lifting myself up, slowly, and carefully so as to not hit my head on a rock, I make way for him to start inching himself upward. As I stand, I have my hand above my head, not wanting to accidentally bash my skull in. My back is still pressed against the slate when a cool breeze brushes the top of my head. I crane my neck to find the slope we slid down. A soft light from the dimming horizon cascades down, illuminating just enough for Seth to see my curves. And for me to see his . . . everything. Gulp.

"You know, as far as adventures go, I'll probably never get another one like this. Especially with a girl." He slides himself up on the rock, standing and facing me.

"Yeah pretty sure you're never going to get a chance to come to the astral planes, much less get a moment like this with me again." I turn, my back toward him now, and try jumping up where the slate curves down but slip, my rear side bumping into him. I quickly move forward, trying to ignore that my ass just touched his dick. God damnit.

"Ouch. I was just saying, despite everything, it's been . . ." He inhales deeply. "I don't know. Exciting."

"Great." Glad you're finding it exciting. "Deacon!" I start calling out. She doesn't answer. We didn't fall that far down. I can see the edge, and just beside it, there's my white bra hanging off a rock. Useless. "We're not going to be able to climb up that slope. It's too steep and wet."

"I saw that. But what we can do is climb on the rocks on this side," he points up to the rock wall opposite the slope. Perfect footholds are in place. Should be an easy climb out if we can reach it.

"How do we reach it though? I'm not strong enough to reach out and pull myself up . . ."

"You'll have to climb on my shoulders and hold on. I'll push you up as far as I can so you can climb out."

"Okay . . . I guess I could try that." I'm not exactly a rock climber.

"You'll have to turn around to get on my shoulders . . ." Ugh. I cover my breasts and slowly turn to face him. The dim lighting hits him from above, softening his features. "Hi."

"Hi," I mutter.

"Okay, ready?" He hovers down a bit so that I could step on his shoulders. I reach out to the walls for support as he slowly lifts himself up. I grab onto the edge of a wall over head with both hands and attempt to do a pull up. Even with him rising, I still can't manage and fall back down.

He grabs me from the waist to keep us from falling on the hard stone again.

"Sorry . . ."

He smiles. "Well, this is cozy." My legs are completely wrapped around his waist and my breasts are fully up against his chest. This is bad. Very, very bad. I quickly drop my legs and cover myself again.

"Are you okay?"

"You mean besides that my bra flew out and now we're stuck like this?"

"I mean, are you hurt?" Despite the awkwardness there is concerned sincerity in his voice. My eyes soften for just a second and my heart throbs. Why does he have to be so freaking good looking? This is so very bad. I shake my head. Okay, think of Ambrose . . . yes, my boyfriend. That's good.

"Addie?"

"Hm? Oh, I scraped my legs and ass a bit, but I'll live."

"Good. In that case, let's try again."

"Ugh. This never happened!"

"Oh, never!" He chuckles.

"Hey! No smiling! No smiling allowed!"

He presses his lips together, not able to hide the two dimples appearing on his cheeks. "Not smiling."

"Mhmm!"

"Uh-uh . . . Nope. Still not smiling." He cracks a smile and blurts out laughing. Despite me being naked, he has surprisingly managed to keep his eyes above my chest. Not that I doubt he's stolen a few looks, but at least he's trying to be a gentleman.

"Hey! This is not funny." He can't contain himself; he has a smile that reaches from cheek to cheek. I huff.

"Oh, come on, it is a little funny."

"No! It is not!" If anything could piss off Ambrose, this would probably be it.

His laughter subsides and his breathing is deep and heavy. I look back up to where I need to go. His eyes bore into me as I do, and I hold my breasts tighter, aware that he is now paying full attention to me. My eyes snap back to his and he's studying my face. I lick my lips, taken aback by the sudden intensity in his eyes.

Our legs are pressed together, not that we have much of a choice in this tight space. My pulse throbs and his cock hardens against my skin. Oh my fucking god.

"I'm ready to get out of here," is all I can think about saying.

He clears his throat. "Yeah . . . Sorry. Let me lift you up this time, and maybe you could reach up higher. When you get a good hold, then step on my shoulders and I stand you up."

"Sounds good." My voice comes out in a whisper and he brings his gaze back down to me.

"Addie?" I swallow hard but keep silent. "I hope that . . . no matter what happens when you find Ambrose, that . . . we can always be friends . . ." My forehead wrinkles.

"Of course, Seth." As long as I can put this awkwardness past me, that is. I should be fine, right? I smile at him and then reach for the rocks while he lifts me up. He's so strong. Okay, concentrate.

I find a good ledge to hold onto and he lifts me up all the way and I find a good foothold to step into. My ass is right on his face now. This just keeps getting better and better. Suddenly, I regret wearing white panties, which are now wet thanks to the water. I reach out to a higher rock. I keep doing that until I climb all the way up, with Seth climbing up after me.

When I get to the top, I have a clear view of the contaminated waters where the evil silverfish inhabit.

My eyes fall on Deacon who has our clothes wrapped in her arms, her brow arched impossibly high.

"Finished playing games?"

"What!? Didn't you see we fell? I was calling you!" Is she serious?

Seth grunts below me as he holds onto the rock. There's a deep gap between where we are and the murky water we have to jump back into. Ugh!

"You both need to hurry up before high tide brings this water back into that hole, taking you too back in with it."

High tide? I didn't think of that. Seth climbs up next to me, holding himself with one arm, while he takes me by the waist with his other.

"What are you doing?"

"Trust me." He lifts me over to the side, close enough for me to jump to where Deacon is. How the hell is he so strong? I land with a splash. If anything bites me, I'll just ignore it. I twist back around and catch a full view of Seth jumping beside me. Be still my heart.

"Deacon, my clothes, now!" Deacon hands me my cloak and I wrap it over myself.

"You best hurry up. Get dressed where it's drier. It's not far from here."

"Oh, thank the gods!" I am over all this water. And the thought of having to put on wet clothes sucks enough. I don't want to have to fight silverfish to put them back on.

"Here, Addie. I was able to reach it for you." Seth hands me my bra.

"Oh shit, thanks!" I'm not sure I'll ever be rid of my burning red cheeks around him after what just happened again. I avert my eyes as we follow Deacon close behind and away from all this water. I get bit a few times but besides me jumping up a little, I try my best to ignore it. The light is almost completely gone, and I do not want to find myself down another chimney shaft type area.

Twenty minutes pass, and the silverfish disperse as the water level lowers. It's becoming easier to walk and I'm at least thankful to be getting out of there. Soon, my ankles are light enough to pick up the pace and my skin is shivering from being naked under my wet cloak.

We find the first dry corner we reach and quickly get dressed. I air out my jeans, hitting them a few times against the stone wall to make sure there isn't anything hiding in them before putting them back on. Wet clothes. This is going to suck.

That orange light didn't last very long. I wonder if we're at the end of the "daylight hours."

I tap Seth's wrist and nudge him to follow me as I quicken my pace to be closer to Deacon. I don't want to take a chance at getting lost again when it's about to get dark, especially since these egregores are more alive than the ones on Earth and can do us harm.

A deafening quiet sweeps over me like a wave and my

ears pop. The gentle scoffing of my feet on the stone floor becomes the only audible thing around and I reach behind me to grab Seth's hand but fall short. I wave my hand around in search of his, then spin backwards. Nothing.

"Seth?" I whisper. "Deacon?" Son of a bitch, how does this keep happening? We were walking in a straight line!

A maniacal laugh erupts from over my head and I duck. Where's that coming from? It starts again. A bodiless head zooms down. It has cracking, white, pasty skin and straw-like red hair. It opens its mouth in a jester grin, but with red shot pupils. I duck again as it aims for my head. Something grabs my arm and pulls me.

"Come on, you have to keep moving."

"Deacon! Where did you go?"

"Nowhere. Your perception will change here, so no matter what, you have to keep walking."

"Where's Seth?"

"Up ahead. I told him to keep walking. He was seeing something different than you."

Oh, this is going to be fun. I roll my eyes and follow her.

"We're cutting through this level so it shouldn't take us long, but it is still a large place. It can take a lot longer if you get caught up in its illusions."

"How would I know which are illusions and which can actually hurt us?"

"You won't."

"Comforting."

I squint my eyes through the ending twilight. How far did Seth get? My chest rumbles and my heart skips a beat, but I ignore it. I'll find Seth first then take my medicine. I have no idea how many hours have passed since the last time I did. My ears pop again. Shit, not again.

Cries coming from a baby echo down the left of the corridor. "A crying baby? In here?"

"Shh," Deacon snaps.

I raise a brow. "Is that an egregore?"

The baby cries louder and my knees shiver. Part of me wants to go see it and make sure it isn't a real baby who needs our help. But another part of me is about ninety-nine percent sure it's an egregore.

"It's Seth!" Deacon says.

My lips part. "What do you mean?" Then it dawns on me: he might be stuck in his own egregore! Shit, I need to get him out. I jog toward the crying, now tantalizing screams and stop when I see an ornate, black crib with a soft light shining from it. A lanky, bald headed demon with its flesh broken in both its cheeks, wearing a red robe with a gold trim emerges from the shadows. What the hell is that hideous thing? I lift my hand up to my mouth as he pokes the baby with what appears to be a hot metal rod and tells it to be quiet. My mouth widens. That's horrible! "Leave that baby alone!" I run over but the demon ignores me. Oh, this is just a reenactment, so they can't hurt us. I think. Maybe don't wake it up.

My eyes fall to Seth, hurdled in the corner, with his back against the wall. His face is buried in his knees, with one eye poking out and staring at the egregores. I push back thoughts from before and run over to him, drop to my knees, and place my hand on his back. "Seth." I nudge him. "Come on, we have to go."

He doesn't move.

"Seth?" He makes himself more rigid and his glossy eyes peek at the scene from between his arms. I flick my eyes to the baby, get up, and walk over to it. I peer into the crib and gasp as the crying baby has two tiny horns on its head and black eyes. Streams of tears fall to the crib from the baby demon's face. His screams of pain rip my insides apart. He's here all alone, no one to care for him. Demon or not, he's just a baby.

The yelling shatters my ear drums and my vision blurs. Ugly with the robe runs back to the crib, carrying its metal rod. I wince at the red-hot coil on the tip of it. Rage sears through my blood as it lets out a raspy wail over the baby's head and flings the rod above his head. Egregore or not, I lose control. I push the demon back, or at least I try to. It doesn't budge. It doesn't even notice me. I can feel it though so it *is* there but it's like it can't feel me. "Leave that baby alone!" I start pounding my fists on its scrawny arms. Just as it swings the rod down, I turn to the baby to grab it but it's too late. Smoke sizzles off of the baby's skin. His little forehead wrinkles and for a split-second, he quiets. Out of shock and fear, no doubt. My heart breaks into a million pieces as its little face shakes, not able to let out a whimper from the pain. I try pushing the demon's arm off the baby but can't. Finally, he lets go and I reach into the crib and grab the crying demon baby.

I hush the infant as I cradle him in my arms. No wonder demons are evil little shits. If they're all treated this way when they're born, what do they expect? I sway back and forth, calming him. The baby stops crying and sniffles. "There, there. It's going to be alright." Would it be possible to take this little guy home with me? I hold him tightly in my arms and flick my eyes up to find Deacon. Do I dare ask her? She'll have my head but I can't just let this baby stay here and be tortured. I won't allow it. "Would you like to come with us?" I whisper to him. My arms suddenly feel weightless.

I gasp. All that's left in my arms is the red blanket it was covered in. I drop it on the ground, my hands shaking. The baby disappeared! I spin around and so has the crib.

Fuck! Was any of this real? I hate the mental plane so much!

Seth stretches his legs in the same place he's been this whole time. "What did you do?" He stretches his neck and rubs his eyes.

"I just picked him up. He just wanted some love. You can't make a baby stop crying by poking it with a hot metal rod. I wasn't sure if it was an egregore or not . . . But that baby, he was being tortured and I couldn't just stand by and watch. Fake or not, human or demon, no one deserves that. And I couldn't get your attention so when I saw what you were looking at, I assumed you were enthralled by the egregore."

Seth doesn't move from his spot. "I don't know. I didn't even see you. It felt like I was frozen, just to stare at that scene, over and over. I don't even know why." He lets out a sad chuckle. "I just felt so sad. I couldn't free myself from it."

"I know the feeling. That's an egregore. I guess it's free game here though. All egregores can affect us. I'm assuming anyway. Let's not get stuck in anyone else's egregores, shall we? Hell, I don't want to get stuck in my own either." I chuckle, trying to break the ice.

"Yeah, let's get out of here," he says, offering me a grin. His eyes are still wet. I don't know why I do it, I guess I just want to comfort him, but I pass my hand through his hair. His eyes lock with mine, and before I pull away, he leans over and kisses my lips. I pull back and gasp.

"Seth . . . I can't. I'm with Ambrose. You know that . . ." My cheeks flush. Just when I thought I'd survived the chimney shaft . . .

He twists his features and grimaces. My stomach clenches. "I'm sorry," he says. "I shouldn't have done that."

He pulls away. "I got caught up in the moment." He gets up. "Let's get out of here."

We meet Deacon at the corner of the corridor and walk in awkward silence. I can't believe he kissed me. Guilt chokes my throat as I think about Ambrose. I'll have to tell him. I don't want any secrets between us. Oh, I could kill Seth. Why did he do that? Especially after . . . the whole naked thing. But it's also not like I've been leading him on. He knows I have a boyfriend! I mean, that's the whole reason we're here! To find my boyfriend! *Okay, just let it go Addie,* I tell myself. He was caught up in the moment. Who knows what he was feeling while he was stuck in that egregore's loop?

I wish I could be with Ambrose right now. I need him to get my mind off Seth. I steal a glance at him from the corner of my eye. He has a stupid smirk on his face. What the hell is *he* thinking about? I'm here torturing myself and he's happy he stole a kiss? Ass.

My ear pops again as the deafening quiet waves over me. Oh fuck, now what? I dart my eyes around and have lost Deacon and Seth. But not really lost them. Remember what Deacon said. Our perceptions change. Just keep moving. I force one slow foot in front of the other as the twilight has now fully gone to bed and it's dark as night once again.

A cold breeze passes through me. The hairs at the back of my neck and arms stand on edge. "Addie?" A familiar voice echoes through the darkness.

I take a few cautious steps forward. "Hello?

"Come here, Addie . . ."

Air catches in my throat as an image emerges a few feet in front of me. His eyes are clouded by a grey film, like what happens to a person when they die. My blood grows cold. "Dad?"

ADDISON

My name slides off his tongue just as it did back in his pocket dimension. Back when I was cursed and didn't know he was my dad. His head bobs over his neck, as if dislocated. I take a step back. I hate that my father went through all that. I wrap my arms around myself. I've suppressed this image ever since Paimon lifted the curse.

"Addie," he starts again, his toes point off the ground, lifting his body, and he barely touches the stone at all. I gasp. His head spins three hundred sixty and I clutch at my stomach, not knowing what to do or where to turn. It's too dark. All I can see is this terrible image that somehow glows bright enough for me to see. I squeeze my eyes shut. "Stop it! Leave me alone, you're not real!"

"Addie." My father's imposter's voice reverberates through my ear drums. I keep my eyes sealed. He isn't real, I tell myself. He isn't real. What if he is? What if he's one of the ones that can hurt me? And then there's silence. Is he gone?

I open my eyes; a soft shriek escapes the back of my

throat. His lips are pulled all the way back, his hair standing at the top of his head. He lets out a long wail and with full speed he flies toward me, his pointed toes just barely touching the floor. I stumble back and fall on my rear. I bury my head in my arms, hoping it'll disappear just like the baby did.

When nothing comes, I lift my head up just a bit but don't see anything out in front of me. But then something touches the top of my head. I duck and arch my head back. There he is, his grey eyes glossing over me. He opens his mouth so wide; I can't see his head anymore. Only a black endless void. He flies down on me, his mouth swallowing me whole. And I scream.

His wailing stops. I'm panting and my hands are shaking, afraid to look up from my knees. My heart thumps in my chest. I'm alive?

"Addison!" Ambrose falls to his knees beside me and I gasp. He wraps his arms around me. "Addison, what happened?"

"H—how . . . how did I get here?"

"A black portal opened up and there you were. What do you remember?"

I shudder and wipe a tear rolling down my cheek.

"Oh, Addie. What happened?"

The image of a demon impersonating my father who tried to swallow me whole shatters my brain. I push it away as fast as I can and I grab for Ambrose.

"I was in the mental plane . . . And . . ."

"Shh, it's okay. I get it. The mental plane can be an awful place."

He tightens his embrace around me, and I sob into his

chest. It should be me comforting him right now, not the other way around. He's the one being kept here as prisoner. *Pull yourself together. It was only an egregore.* I swallow my angst, refusing to shed any more tears for a stupid illusion. He wipes a rebel tear away and I press my face on his chest and point my chin up. His chin meets my forehead and my lips find his.

He nibbles on my bottom lip and my hand caresses his chest. He pulls me in closer and I climb on top of his legs. He takes my tongue in his mouth, sucking it gently. My spine tingles and an image of Seth kissing me disrupts my bliss.

I gasp and pull away.

"What's wrong?"

"Nothing. I—" I climb off of him and let out a long sigh, holding my head in my hand.

"Addison?"

"My friend who followed me here kissed me. I didn't kiss him back. He had been stuck in an egregore loop and I guess he got caught up in the moment when I tried to comfort him."

"I see."

"I'm sorry, Ambrose. I didn't mean for that to happen. I . . ." My pulse quickens and my mind grows fuzzy.

"Addison, it's okay. I know you didn't mean it. The mental plane is a complicated place. Just make sure you get out of there soon, okay? The faster you get out of there, the faster you can get to the Akashic and get me out of here."

My lip trembles and I give him a single nod. "Okay."

He pushes himself closer to me. "It's been too long without you, Addison. Come back," he says, pulling me into him.

A soft chuckle escapes my throat. "I'm sorry, I just

wasn't expecting to be here. I thought I was a goner, you know?"

"The one thing I learned from being here is to seize every unexpected, good thing that falls in your lap. Because you never know when it'll be gone, and if it'll ever happen again. Just be with me now. Let's enjoy each other's company while we have it."

"You're right. Before they come for me again. God, I hate Azazel. I feel like he's just toying with me. Why can't he just send me a portal to the Akashic already?"

"You can't just appear at the Akashic. You already know that, silly."

I quirk an eyebrow at him. "Yeah, I know, *silly*."

"You know what I've been thinking about lately?"

"What?"

His face grows red and he darts his eyes away.

"Ambrose, what is it? Tell me."

"Well, the last time you were here got me thinking, What if I never get out of here?"

My eyes flare. "Don't say that."

He grabs my hands. "No, listen. I'm just saying I know we both want our first time to be special. But . . . This cell is technically in the mental plane. What we think, we can make a reality."

"What are you saying? Like, can we change our surrounding? Wouldn't Azazel find out?"

"Who cares if he does? He knew this was a conjugal visit, didn't he?"

That's true. I blush and look down at my hands pressing on the stone. "I don't want to think of the possibility of not getting you out of here."

"And have you put any thought to what you're going to do about releasing the devil out of his cage?"

My eyes widen. Admittedly, with everything I've been

through in the last several hours, I forgot about that teeny detail. I shake my head.

"So, you don't really know what's going to happen, do you?"

I sigh. "No, but I'll figure something out."

He leans in and kisses me. "I know you will. And I'm not trying to pressure you. I just thought you might want to also. Being trapped in here has given me a lot of time to think . . ."

"Oh, I do . . . Ambrose, I really do. You have no idea," I chuckle and look down again. "I'm just conflicted, you know? This is a prison. And we're on a mission." Not that I'm letting anything else get in the way of it. Like considering how this relationship is actually going to work, long-term. Because I'm totally not.

"It doesn't have to look like a prison. It's not something you can permanently alter, but for a short time, it won't look like this."

"I get it. It takes effort to hold an appearance. It's more than that though. Would it be . . . right for us?"

He peers into my eyes. "There are no rules."

This is true. Maybe I am willing to throw out any conventions I may have had of a perfect date. What if he's right and we don't get another chance? "I'll think about it."

"Only if it's what you want as well," he says with a smile. I lean in for another kiss when a revitalizer emanates from the wall and swooshes from behind. I gasp, holding out my hand that is still touching his, until his image becomes smoke. And dissipates.

"GHOST RIDERS IN THE SKY"

DAX

Open flames block the hut's only exit. How long was I out? The shaman woke me right before making a dash to safety. I wouldn't have wanted him to wait for me. I'm dead. I can't get hurt but he can. I bolt through the roaring fire just as a piece of the roof caves in behind me. Outside, the villagers have spread out, arming themselves and ushering their children away. Their warriors are in the front lines, fighting their attackers. I skim the village huts, making sure no one is dead or dying.

I spot the woman who had beckoned her son away from me earlier running at me, her eyes pleading. "*Mi hija,*" she repeats frantically, grabbing my arm and pointing at one of the huts that have caught fire, presumably from a burning arrow. Oh shit. Her daughter is stuck inside. Freeing myself from her grasp, I run into the hut as fast as I can. Debris falls from the ceiling, blocking my sight. I turn just as a piling from the roof falls onto my arm. I need to work fast. Cries from the end of the room spark a hint of hope. I nearly topple over as I climb over what I think are broken chairs to find her hiding under a table, covered with ashes. Shaken and withdrawn, she whimpers, clearly too afraid to move. I reach my hand out and she shakes her head. We don't have time for this. A piece of the ceiling falls on her opposite side and she scrambles over to me. I reach in and pick her up. "Easy now. I'll get you out of here."

The fire is closing in, blocking my view of the exit. Another piling falls right in front of us and the little girl screams. I'm going to have to make a run for it. I embrace her to shield her head from the scorching flames. I leap over the fallen debris and make it to the outside. The little girl's mother runs toward us and wraps her arms around her.

I urge them to get up and run to the shaman who is helping to keep others safe. Groups of men and women are running with buckets of water to try and extinguish the fire. I want to help but I turn toward the battle that is happening at the center of the village. This is where I need to be. Who would do such a thing to these people? Wishing I had my scythe, I search for something I can use as a weapon.

My wish is granted when an arrow pierces my chest. I look up at a man riding a horse, his face covered in blue paint. I give him a broad grin, grip onto the hilt of the arrow, and pull it straight out of my chest. The man's horse backs away, but the warrior fights to keep the reins straight as blood drains from his face. I turn the arrow and aim it right at the man, power coursing through me. The last thing the man sees before the arrow pierces him is a fire blazing in my eyes. He falls off his horse and lands face down on the ground.

What will the High Council do to me once they find out I have broken a sacred rule and taken a life? I shake the thoughts from my mind. The raiders need to be stopped. I'll deal with the repercussions later.

Despite not having my scythe, the power that surges through my bones is like none I've ever felt. It's as if something inside me has unlocked. I walk straight into the battle, fearless and godlike. Some of the invaders that witnessed what happened turned and ran. Others steady their weapons and aim them at me. This time, gunshots are fired. The warriors have upped their game, leaving their heavy ammunition for last. No matter how many shots are fired at me, I keep walking, disarming them one by one, trying not to kill if I don't have to.

Seeing the villagers I had met before lying injured or dead on the ground sends the flames that lit up in my eyes surging down through the veins in my arms. My hands catch flames, then the rest of my arms, and finally my face. This is certainly new and unexpected, but I'll think on it later. Right now . . . I turn my head slowly to a man ordering his men to fall back. Their leader, I gather. I lift my hand as a threat to catch *them* all on fire with a single throw. See how they like it.

The warriors stop shooting and fighting, I stand my ground, making sure that every last one of them has gone.

The fire that had covered my body so easily, and unburning, vanishes. That was . . . exhilarating. Holy shit.

I spin around, slowly; eyes fixed on the fallen villagers that are bleeding on the forest floor. So many of them. They did not deserve to die like this. I reach down and lift one of the village warriors that has an arrow sticking out from his stomach. I carry him back to the huts, others doing the same and following me closely behind. The ones still standing lay their fallen comrades down on the ground, underneath a shaded area in their community center. The brother of the girl I had saved from the fire runs toward us. I swallow hard, hoping to God that their father isn't one of the ones dying. They run past me and hug a man that has just helped to set down an injured tribesman.

Xiomara places her hand on my back, and I turn to face her. She draws me in close and gives me a hug, squeezing me tight. "Thank you," she says with a tear rolling down her face.

"Who were they?"

She lets go and wipes her face. "Illegal loggers and drug traffickers, wanting to clear us out of their way. We're leaving here anyway, heading East." She points toward the mountains. "If it weren't for you, I think they would have killed everyone. They outnumbered us and caught us off guard. Don't let their blue paint fool you. They do that to get past the town, making everyone think that they are us, and then they attack. Many of us thought you were going to bring turmoil. Some thought you did this, but now they think you were sent to help. Like a prophecy. I always knew you were good."

I shake my head and place a hand on her shoulder. A surge of power grows in my chest, as if urging me toward the fallen, to collect their souls. I need to help these people pass on. But without my scythe, I don't know how I can. "What about them?" I point to the injured.

"They are alive but suffering. I will tend to their wounds; the ayahuasca will help."

Natural medicine isn't going to help this time. "What about hospitals? Medical centers?"

"We are too remote. Not enough time."

I walk around the area. If some of these people are dying, a reaper will come soon to collect them. A spark of hope lifts my spirits. Once the reaper arrives, I'll go back and deal with whatever is going on with my sister. I crane my neck back out to the field toward the man I killed. But why hasn't anyone come yet? Did I miss them during the fight? Surely, a reaper would have seen me and stopped me, brought me back to face the council?

Something lands on my shoulder. It's Digo. He must have climbed up the trees at the start of the fight. "Hey, little buddy. I bet you miss your friend." He chatters back and I look around for the little girl. The familiar sound of vents spinning behind me make me turn on my heel. Digo runs off as a portal opens and a woman with red hair, wearing a black robe, steps out.

"I was starting to think I'd never see you again," I say.

The look in Deacon's eyes tells me she feels the same. The portal closes behind her. "You came to me, didn't you?"

"Yes. Hours ago. Well . . . last night at this point. I was invited to sit in a ceremony. The moment I touched a plant the shaman gave me I felt my soul go back to the astral plane. Why were you chained up?"

"It's a long story. I have to get you out of here."

"Deacon, my scythe was taken from me. And Ambrose, he's been—"

"I know. I know everything." She lowers her head slightly. "None of us have our scythes. The reapers are under attack."

"Under attack? What do you mean?" So, it wasn't just about Ambrose.

"We really need to go. I'll explain on the way, but we have to move fast."

I rub the back of my neck. "Alright, just give me a chance to say goodbye. These people have gone through hell. We had a war and I helped—"

Deacon's eyes widen. "A war? How many deaths have occurred here?"

"None so far. I think they'll survive. This could have gone a lot worse." I tense my muscles in hesitation. "Except, I killed one."

Deacon's frown deepens. "Where is the body?"

I point toward the field.

"He is still alive, just suffering in agony."

"What, why? No, he couldn't have survived."

"No reapers mean no deaths. Only pain and suffering. The Judge is working on freeing the others. I'll take care of this one, but I need you to come back with me."

I clench my hand into a fist. "But what about Ambrose?"

"The Judge doesn't want to help him. Dax, he found out about Ambrose and your sister. We saw him through the Akashic waters, Azazel made him human."

I remember the sigil the demon carved on Ambrose's chest before he was pushed into the portal. "Where is he?"

"In a desert somewhere, possibly dying. The Judge says we'll see him again on the other side, but I have a sinking feeling that he won't let that happen. If Ambrose does die, he'll suffer until one of us collects him, but we won't have a say in his fate. I doubt we'll see him again."

Even though there isn't a fight erupting around me, the news ignites a flame of rage in my gut. I fight to suppress it. "Deacon, you have to let me find him and bring him back. Let him speak for himself if he's still alive. He did so much for me, I can't go on knowing he's not safe."

She arches a brow and gives me a knowing smile and I can tell she's attuned to what is going on inside of me. "What else happened?"

Right, the psychic thing. "Something did happen, but Deacon . . . Ambrose. Let's worry about me later."

She sighs and drops her shoulders. "We'll talk about that later. We don't know if Ambrose is still alive. And there are implications . . . of him losing his immortality. The Akashic knowledge is too vast for a human to bear. He could be losing his memory of being a reaper. Or the Judge could have taken care of him already. Come back with me and we'll find out." I know she doesn't want to disobey orders, but we can't just forget about Ambrose!

"Deacon, please. Open the portal to his location. You know you can do that. If he's not in the desert, then I'll go back with you. You know Ambrose. What would he do if it were one of us?"

I detect a hint of softness in Deacon's eyes. She nods. "I'll cover for you, but make it back, soon. We really need you."

"Thank you. How will I get back?"

The shaman, who was tending to the injured nearby, steps forward. "When you touched the ayahuasca, you went somewhere else. Your body was here, but maybe if you eat it, it'll work the same way. The Earth is filled with many mysteries and leavings of your kind." He holds the vine, covered in a cloth, out in front of us.

Deacon takes the vine and smells it. "Yes, this is used as a glimpse between worlds for humans. It might be able to transport you, but it will work differently. If it has enough power to open a portal, you'll have to use it sparingly. Think of exactly where you want to go, and it can direct you. If there's not enough left, you could become trapped between realms, so be cautious."

I take the cloth and turn to face the shaman. "Thank you. You have helped me more than you know."

"It is you who has helped us."

I place a hand on his shoulder and smile. Deacon nods and opens a portal to the Sahara Desert.

Just before I step through, I turn to her. "Do me a favor?"

Deacon raises her eyebrows.

"Tell my sister I'm okay? And that I'm going to find her foolish boyfriend. She'll be worried that we never showed."

Deacon scoffs but then smirks, nodding again in agreement.

I MIGHT HAVE TO RELEASE THE DEVIL

ADDISON

"Well? What did he say?" Deacon's grimace is the only thing reflecting from the eve of the orange lighting above our heads. I can't bear to call it the next day already. My eyelids are heavy and my muscles ache as I lean against the wall, struggling to hold myself up while staring at her.

"He only said that we don't know how we can get him out of there if I don't know what I'm going to do about my end of the deal with Azazel." I'm obviously not going to tell them about everything else we talked about . . .

"And? Have you considered what you're going to do about opening the cage?"

"Me? I thought we were going to figure that out together."

Deacon crosses her arms. "Well, you're not going to be able to deceive him, you know."

"What are you getting at?"

"Addison, I fear that you will have to unlock that cage."

And as if a jolt of electricity shot up my ass, I'm awake. "You know I can't do that." Am I hearing her correctly?

Deacon, the Goody Two-shoes reaper, wants me to open the devil's prison? And let him out? I flick my gaze over to Seth, who is standing quietly with his eyes glued to the floor. What is up with him? He'd usually be telling me something like, there's no way in hell I can do that, blah blah.

"All I'm saying is you might not have a choice."

I swallow. I'm spending too much time thinking about my meetups with Ambrose. Deacon's right. I need to figure out a plan. I might not have a choice and then what? What's the worst that can happen if I release the devil? "How long until we get to the Akashic?"

"Not long now. We're almost out of the mental plane, and then we'll be there."

"Great, let's get going then, shall we?" Seth says and I quirk a brow at him.

"Are you doing okay?" I whisper to him.

"I'm fine, Addison. Just tired of being in this area." His eyes drift past us and the sadness in them reminds me of the crying baby.

"Yeah, you're right. Let's go. Deacon, show the way." She spins on her heel and leads us down the same path we were on, except now the corridor is going back to being narrow and descending. I watch my footing as the path becomes steeper. Images of demons start forming on the stone as they did when we first got to LLAPS. "Deacon? How come things are starting to look like before? Are we going around in a circle?"

"No, we're at a crossings."

I scrunch up my forehead.

"The maze, remember?" Seth says.

"Oh yeah, that makes sense."

Up ahead looks as if we're climbing down an endless dark pit. My stomach drops as I'm afraid I might miss a step and plummet to my death. A rumble comes from behind us.

Nerves spring up in my gut as I'm suddenly pressured to pick up the pace down a steep hill. "Deacon, what the hell is happening?"

"Addison, move to the side!" Seth shouts. Rocks fall over me, a few hitting my back. One hits my head. I crane my neck and nearly choke. A large boulder the size of a building crushes a naked demon, who tries to hold it back from falling all the way down.

"There's nowhere to go!" I yell.

Seth pushes me down as he lands on top of me. The boulder flies over us and dissipates.

"What the hell? Was that an egregore?" I say, getting up from under him while trying to maintain my balance.

"Get down!" Seth pushes me back down as he springs to his feet. A long blade nearly takes off his head, but he ducks and kicks a man's kneecaps, causing them to break in half. My eyes widen as he falls down the steep archway. I try to look back at Deacon when I catch a glimpse of another figure emerging from the hill. Is that a reaper? It swings its blade toward Seth, aiming for his head. Why are reapers after him?

A rumble starts from the hill again. I duck as I catch Seth blocking the blade, twisting the reaper's arm with the same arm, and disarming him. With the same blade, he swings it back and dismembers the reaper. Holy shit, he's good. But why are reapers after him?

"They're not real, Addison!" Deacon shouts. "Come down here! That boulder is about to drop!"

But I can't hear her over the sound of the boulder rolling toward me. My whole life flashes before my eyes as it crashes down over me, flinging me down with it. I fall and slide down the slate stones as they get steeper and steeper. The demon carvings on the wall open up their mouths wide and hold out their claws as if trying to help me. My fingers try desperately to grab on, but I pick up too much speed. I don't have time to scream. Before I know it, I'm hitting the bottom fast when all of a sudden a hand grabs my arm.

My heart jumps out of my chest as Seth grips on tightly. With immeasurable strength he pulls me up and I get hold of my balance. He sets me down gently next to the stone wall.

"H-how did you get to me so fast?" I say.

"I have fast reflexes." He lets out a breath, a dimple appearing on his left cheek.

"The reapers weren't real?"

"No," Deacon says. "But they were the kind of egregores that can kill us."

"Why would egregores be in the form of killer reapers?"

"Back when the reapers and demons were at war with each other. Some egregores were created from war, Addison."

I take a deep breath. "Right."

"I just saw blades coming for my head and I started swinging," Seth says, with another smirk, trying to make me feel better.

"Well, I'm sorry you were the one they went after. Although, strange as that is."

He shrugs. "Are you okay?"

"Honestly? I really thought I was going to die." I look down. It's a long way down.

"Well, glad you didn't." He says.

I scoff. "Yeah, me too." I climb to my feet but my heart has skipped several beats since my fall. I rub my knees and backside. That couldn't have been good for me.

Ambrose's words ring through my mind. What if I don't get him out? What if I don't get to see him again? I almost just died.

"Ready to keep going?" Deacon says.

"Actually, you two keep going. I want to see Ambrose." Seth hardens his face. "What? *Now?*"

"I know, I'm sorry. It's just he was scared of us not being able to see each other again. And just now my whole life flashed before my eyes . . ." If not just to tell him I love him.

He pinches the bridge of his nose and holds it for a second. "Addison—I just saved your life. Again. What else do I need to do to prove to you that I'm your better option?"

My eyebrows raise and I drop my hands to my sides. Better option? Are you kidding me right now? "Seth, thank you for saving my life but . . . I am still with Ambrose. And I am still here to save *Ambrose.*" What? Did he think I was just going to realize that he's been the right one for me, and drop my boyfriend?

"He's a reaper, Addison. You'll never be able to have a family with him. You'll never be at peace with him either because he'll be taking off on you for unforeseeable amounts of time. He's not right for you, Addie . . . Why can't you see that?"

I stare blankly at him. I know he's right. But it doesn't matter to me. I know what my heart wants . . .

"How do you know he even feels love?"

I exhale shakily.

"He can't *really* love you. He's dead." I shake my head.

"No . . . not dead. He was created . . ."

"Even worse. He was created to be some sort of robot. A hollow, soulless entity wearing a human meat suit to collect souls. You don't even know *what* he is." His voice is icy. My lower lip trembles.

"You don't know that. He's developing emotions. I know Ambrose has feelings for me."

Seth scoffs. "It was probably all for curiosity's sake, him being with you."

"What the hell Seth?" Now my voice is raising. "How dare you say that to me? You don't know shit and right now, I can't deal with this. My boyfriend—who, by the way, also saved me once—is depending on me. And right now, after I almost just lost my life, I want to see him."

Seth's chest heaves and so does mine. I steal a quick glance toward Deacon, who is standing quietly in a corner of rubble, trying to make herself scarce.

"You and I will never be together, Seth. I love Ambrose. I'm sorry."

Seth's eyes soften and lifts his chin. "Fine. I get it."

"Seth . . ."

He holds up a hand. "Go be with your man, Addison."

I twist around, ignoring his gaze searing into my back. Forget him. How do I get a revitalizer's attention? They usually just show up. Then through the walls, one emerges. I knew there was some sort of connection between what I need and what comes to me here.

"I'll just have it drop me off wherever you two end up."

Seth nods. Just before I step into the giant hole of the revitalizer, a little knowing twinkle reflects from Seth's eye.

"Ambrose?" I spot him curled in the corner with his head between his legs. The revitalizer merges through the wall and leaves us alone. Ambrose perks up.

"Addison!"

I run to him. "Are you alright?"

"I am now. What made you come back so soon?"

I take a deep breath and tell him how I almost met my untimely death. "At least I'm already here, right? It wouldn't be a long trip."

"Don't make jokes like that."

"Sorry." I push myself to his face and kiss his warm lips.

"I'm just happy you're back."

"Me too," I say, letting my hands wander his body.

He quirks an eyebrow. "Addie? What are you doing?"

I know a lot has happened, but I really want to be here in the present moment with him. Right or wrong, I don't care. If not now, then when? And what if we don't get another chance? I push him to the wall, and he flings his arms back.

"Woah, Addie! What's gotten into you?"

"I want you."

"Now? But you said . . ."

"I don't care what I said. You're right. There's no better time than the present. The fact that I almost lost my life made me miss you more, and made me afraid of . . ."

"Shhh . . . It's okay, Addie. But wait."

"Wait for what?"

He presses his finger to my lips. "Close your eyes."

I close my eyes, a smile sliding on my face. I can't believe we're doing this. Here. Now. "Ambrose, this is crazy."

"Shh. Keep them closed."

"I am."

"Okay, now open them."

When I open my eyes, a gentle gasp escapes my lips. The cell is no longer an ugly grey block. A tall bed with pillars on each corner decorates the middle of the room, silk red and gold sheets neatly made. Birds sing as the room has opened up to the mauve skies of LLAPS, and I'm standing on grey grass with silky glass flowers. My eyes land on a bush of black roses like the one Azazel had left in my bedroom, but I shake off the image. Not now. They're just flowers.

Ambrose motions forward, extending his hand out to me. I smile and take it as he brings me closer to the tall bed. He moves my hair back from my shoulders and unclasps my cloak. I let it fall by my feet as he moves his hands up my shirt, feeling my skin. I help him with my bra and he draws me in closer and kisses my neck. I close my eyes, trying to be here in the present. I almost died an hour ago. I want to be here. I want to do this. I hurry with the rest of my clothes and tug softly on his.

He wraps his hands around my waist and helps me

jump up on the bed. The silk sheets slide beneath my skin as I slip myself under the covers. I watch as he removes his clothes.

"Are you sure we'll be safe doing this here?" I ask.

"Shhh . . . It'll be fine. Just be with me," he says and presses his lips against mine before I can say okay.

He climbs on top of me and lowers himself, exposing his clavicle right over my lips. I nibble on his skin, kissing him as he presses himself against my core. I close my eyes and my knee moves up as I squeeze his body into mine. I moan as he enters me. His breath quickens as we both move rhythmically. My spine tingles as he thrusts his hips into mine and my eyes blink open as I pass my fingers through his hair.

I gasp. The room has changed. We're back in my bed, the texture of the sheets beneath my body has also changed and the light is coming from my window on the right. I close my eyes again, letting him keep going, I don't want it to stop.

He thrusts back and forth, and I moan louder. I open my eyes and the room has changed again to Ambrose's quarters. We're in his low bed. Is he doing this or am I? I can change the scene here too, can't I? Okay, shut up. I don't want to thi—

He squeezes my skin with his fingers as he moans. I move my lips up to his and bite down on his lower lip. My vulva contracts and releases and we both moan with him still inside of me. I squeeze my eyes shut, my heart panting in unison with his. I open them and let out a scream. Fire fumes all around us. The heat from the flames scorches my skin. He doesn't seem to notice as he climaxes. Horns emerge from the top of his head, his physical appearance changing before me. I jerk back as he finishes.

"Ambrose? What the fuck?" I move my legs up. "Get off me!"

He screws up his face, taken aback that I yelled at him. He looks at his arms and shakes his body. His appearance comes back. He's Ambrose again. Is he? ". . . Y–you changed."

"I don't know why. It must have been effects from the mental plane."

"You looked just like Azazel," I spit. This is too weird. What if . . . I shudder to think. Oh my gods, what if he's been Azazel, fooling me this whole time?

He moves closer and places his hand on top of mine, but I jerk it away.

"Addison! Please don't . . . It's me, Ambrose, I promise."

"How can I be sure? You changed physical form! Isn't Azazel magical?"

"Yes, but we're in the mental plane. Maybe it was Azazel doing that to me on purpose to confuse you!"

I snap my mouth shut. I guess that's possible. I don't want to consider the unthinkable. I edge myself to the corner of the bed and he rushes to help me down.

"Stop, I can get down myself."

"Addie, you're going to stay mad? It's just this place. I'm really me, I promise."

I put my hand up. "I know. I just . . . can't think clearly right now. It was too real." I quickly get dressed and the room changes as soon as I pull my shirt over my head. We're back in the cell and a dark portal is waiting for me to leave. I turn to him one last time. "I just need to think things through. If you're really Ambrose, I'll get you out of here." He nods and I turn and step through the revitalizer's portal. If he's not, then I think I'll find a fire pit and jump in it.

YOU KNOW I'M A BAD ASS

DEACON

S trapped and ready, with scythe in hand, I open a portal and step into the ransacked courtroom. The Judge should have released the rest of the High Council by now and hopefully has come up with a plan for our next move. That bastard Azazel is pretending to be me. Even if the Judge doesn't care to help Addison, I won't turn my back on her. Not when Dax and Ambrose would want me to keep her safe. I'm the only one who can help her now. The only thing is, how am I going to do that with the Judge breathing over my shoulder?

It looked like she was headed toward the prison when I saw her in the water. That's where I'll go first.

Broken chairs and tables are piled on top of each other. Among them are shattered bones and torn fabric belonging to my fallen comrades. I hold my breath as my eyes scan the battle scene. Seeing that the room is empty, I step out of the shadows. My eyes circle around, remembering the last time I was here. I scoff; no time for trips down memory lane. I turn toward the exit, picking up my pace, careful not to make a sound.

I know my way around the corridors like the back of my hand. But with all the extra guardsmen working for Azazel around, I need to watch myself. The Judge was right before: we can't take our normal routes. I move fast, hiding behind corners, cautious not to be seen. Sounds of dripping water grow louder the lower I go. The astral levels form an infinity symbol, each level ending in a loop that connects to the level below. If I can cut through the Akashic level, I can make it down to where the prison is kept, closer to where the lower astral beings come from.

I press my back against the stone wall and slide along it, blending in with the darkness. I inch back, holding my breath as a guardsman crosses in front of me, the padding footsteps echoing behind him. I wait until he's a few inches away. When he passes me, I lift my scythe and jam it into his back. It jerks from side to side, but I keep a firm grip. Pushing it in deeper, I'm able to bring the guardsman to his knees. I pull the scythe out from his back and kick him down to the ground. No need for magick here. Leaping over the monstrous figure, I bend down to grab the ax and continue on my way.

As the Akashic level comes into view, so many uncertainties run through my mind. What if everyone has already been captured? What if the Judge is captured, and everyone is still blacked out in their cells? I need to strategize. The only safe place is the Akashic level, as reapers are the only ones allowed to go in and out freely. No demon is ever allowed to enter. My breath escapes my body. Except for Azazel.

As the original angel of death, surely he could go in freely? Could that access have been taken away when the Judge imprisoned him? If the Judge had made it in, then there would be reapers waking up, magick most likely in use, and guards everywhere. Enough of this sneaking around. I have to go now.

I take out the pocket scythe, open a portal, and step through to the prison. I hide the scythe in the folds of my cloak and grip onto the ax. I cover my head with my hood and slowly walk around the wall. A revitalizer stands in front of iron gates. How did the Judge get in? That gate is too narrow. I'm not sure how I'm going to bypass the revitalizer. If I use the scythe, I risk losing it. Maybe if I use it from this distance, wipe out the revitalizer . . . No. I'd be risking dozens, if not hundreds, of revitalizers coming out of the shadows to devour me. *Shit.* I hold back for a few moments to see if it turns or moves, but it doesn't. I need to try. It's now or never.

"Psst."

I freeze, holding the scythe above my head.

"What are you doing? Put that down, you buffoon."

I look behind me but don't see anyone. "Who's that whispering?"

"Up here."

I arch my head to the Judge glaring down at me from a window. I sigh with relief, but I'm also annoyed. What is he still doing here? How am I going to rescue Addison?

"Get up here, quickly. Give me your hand."

I reach up and grab his hand as he helps pull me through the arched window. "I am relieved to see you're alive, Your Honor. I was worried. How did you get past the revitalizer down there?"

"I knew that some of these cells have barred windows and was prepared to come through them." The Judge looks around and behind me. "Where's Dax?"

My hand trembles as I stick it inside my cloak. "He'll be right behind me," I lie. "There was a war where I collected him, and I needed to reap the fallen and suffering. I told him to secure the levels before the Akashic in case I couldn't find you, or I didn't make it back." I swallow. "I thought we could use a strong reaper out there in case none of us make it back."

"You left him there defenseless?"

I hold up the ax. "With one of these, we took down two guardsmen."

The Judge eyes me for a moment and then relaxes. "Good thinking, Deacon. It's wise to have someone outside of the prison, just in case. But he'll need instructions on what to do should the circumstance arise that—"

"He's resourceful, Your Honor. I trust that he will do the right thing."

He nods and turns to face the open entryway. "We should go. There isn't much time. I released a good dozen, and they are releasing the others. We need to make it back inside the Akashic plane. I have been waiting for you to bring me my scythe. I will need it to create a pocket dimension, where it will be safe enough for us to plan our next steps."

I hand over his scythe and follow him out the door.

Making it back up the level is easier than I expected. The Judge leads us up a cleaner path, having already been taken care of mostly by himself and my cohorts while I was away. The astral plane is an utter mess, but we make it through unnoticed. Could Azazel already be aware of the breach?

The Judge lifts his scythe and whispers words I can't hear. The blade gives off a blue shine and a portal appears.

"Come inside, Deacon. We'll wait here and watch for the others."

"I'll be right in. Just going to scry in these waters for a bit. I'll direct anyone who comes." The Judge fixes his jaw and repeats the one thing he always tells me. I resist the urge to roll my eyes.

"Be mindful over the waters, Deacon. You of all should know that past, present, and future are not always shown at their correct time. They can be unreliable." He steps through and closes the pocket dimension.

I need some time alone to check on Dax and Ambrose, but first, where the hell are Addison and Azazel?

My hands are shaking as I step back onto the stone corridor floor. Seth is up ahead with Deacon, but I take my time to get to them. I don't know if I can pretend everything is okay and carry on with the mission. Did I just have sex with Azazel? Did he really trick me? Or was it Ambrose? My eyes well up. Come to think of it, Ambrose was acting strange, wasn't he? Seemed more . . . confident. How could I tell?

Seth calls out to me, but I ignore him. Images of Ambrose turning into Azazel flash before my eyes. The way he touched me . . . What if it wasn't really him? What do I do? My throat closes and I clutch my stomach.

But then again, what if it was Ambrose, and Azazel was trying to confuse me? But why? How would that make me help him? I wouldn't do it. The deal would be off. So then, if it wasn't an illusion . . . then that means . . . it was real? My vision blurs as nausea sweeps over me and my stomach constricts. I force my bile down my throat but it's too late. I lurch forward and sink to my knees. My stomach clenches violently as white liquid spews from my throat. I cough as sweat and tears roll down my face.

"Addison!" Seth runs over and holds my hair back.

"I'm okay," I say, sniffling. The pungent stench invades my nostrils as pain strikes at my throat from dry heaving after not having eaten anything in hours, or days.

Seth rubs my back and I push him back, embarrassed by the smell. "I'm fine. Let's go."

"Are you sure? Maybe Deacon can find you some water," he says loud enough for Deacon to hear. She disappears into what I assume is another hidden room in the walls.

I nod. "Yeah, okay." I refrain from telling him what I'm upset about. He'll want to leave immediately if he thinks I may have just been played by Azazel. Not to mention, he's jealous enough as it is. This will just drive him crazy . . . I need to know the truth. My suspicion isn't enough for me. There's only one way to know the truth, and that's to make it to the Akashic. Forget asking the waters how to save Ambrose, I want to know if he's really imprisoned here, if that was really him I slept with, and if not, where the hell is he and how do I get him out?

I rub my face with the corner of my shirt. "How was your journey down here?" I ask, trying to take the focus off of me. Besides, I need a distraction to keep going.

Seth shrugs. "Fine, I guess. Ran into some revitalizers. But nothing too spectacular."

I nod and scrunch up my features. How is it that Seth is not affected by revitalizers but is by egregores? They both draw out emotions. Well, I guess technically egregores can be from anyone. Maybe he really doesn't have much baggage. In the time I'd known him, I never asked him about his past. I guess I always assumed he was a bit of a playboy and I never felt the need to pry into his business.

I turn my head to stare at the dark abyss of the corridor. I can't shake the feeling that something terrible is about to happen. Footsteps creep up behind us, sending shivers down my spine. I spin around to face a dark figure hovering over us.

I let out a long sigh as Deacon emerges from the darkness holding a glass goblet of water.

Seth puts his hand on my shoulder and rubs it.

"I'm just jumpy," I say while taking the goblet from Deacon. "Thank you."

I gulp down the last drop, then realize I hadn't offered any water to Seth. "There's more drinkable water where we're going," Deacon says.

"How far are we from there? I'm sorry, Seth. I didn't realize how thirsty I was."

He chuckles. "No, that's fine. I'm not the one who just puked my brains out." My features slacken and I offer him a half smile. His tone is back to normal with me and I know he's trying his hardest to be here for me while probably still shaken by our argument. I can't even think about our argument right now.

"We're not far, but this time, please, stay close."

I walk in silence beside Seth, trying to avoid thinking about Azazel, unless I want to vomit again. I'm just so angry. How could I be so stupid? I keep getting deceived.

"Penny for your thoughts?"

I glance at Seth and sigh. "It's just that so much has happened to me, I guess I never took the time to reflect, until now. My ex-boyfriend was, er, you'll think this is totally insane, but he was a manipulation sent by a demon to keep me away from my family."

"Wait, what? What do you mean a manipulation?"

"I mean he wasn't a real person. I fell in love with a creature in disguise. All because a demon wiped my memory and wanted to keep me away from my dad so that it could feed off him."

"Addison, if I hadn't followed you and a reaper through a portal, I wouldn't believe that story."

"I know it sounds crazy. Which is why I pushed it from my mind. I mean, I didn't have anyone to talk to. Except for my best friend, Ava, but I guess I felt stupid for falling in love with an avatar. I didn't want to think about it, you know?"

"I know what you mean."

"You dated an avatar demon that pretended to love you, too?" My voice cracks, but I suppress the urge to laugh.

"Well, no, not exactly that. But I've experienced deception and pain." His eyes glaze over.

"Oh, I'm sorry. Do you want to talk about it?"

"Not really . . ."

I place my hand on his shoulder. "I understand. If you ever do want to talk, know that I'm here for you." I'll just leave it at that, considering the last time I tried to talk to him he snapped at me.

"I've always tried to be the best at everything. I work with my hands, and I've always aimed for perfection. Always at the top of my game, and I'm well versed in history, literature, math, science, you name it."

"Yeah, I've noticed you're quite the Renaissance man. So, what's the problem?"

"He never told me he was proud of me."

"Who?"

"And all I ever wanted was to be a good son."

"Oh, your father." Poor guy is still looking for his father's approval. My eyes drift to the side. Maybe that's why he was so affected by the crying baby demon.

"I've always had to be the one to pick up after his mess-es." Seth's voice rises. "Because he has no one else. Just me, and I can't help it that I love my old man, even though he didn't have much time for me as a kid."

"What about your mom?"

He shakes his head and looks at me. "No, no mom."

"Oh, I'm so sorry Seth. I never knew."

"She died when she had me."

I take his hand in mine and squeeze it. He smiles back.

"Well, what do you say that from now on, we can lean on each other when we want to get something off our chest?"

"I'd really like that, Addison. I don't really have people I confide in either."

My lips curl upward. "I didn't mean I didn't have people to confide in. I do. I'd just rather not discuss past loves with my boyfriend, and I don't want my brother to worry about me."

I've been through a lot with Ambrose and I love him, but there are some things he can't relate to as a reaper. And there's no way in hell I'm confessing *that* to Seth.

"Oh, I didn't mean to offend you, Addison. I just mean that *I* don't have people I can lean on."

My cheeks flush red. "Oh, right. Sorry." Cool it Addie, I'm still just worked up. I'm trying to get my mind off of things, not make it worse. I realize I'm still holding his hand. I let it go and wrap my arms around my waist. The temperature is dropping again as we near a misty area in the corridor with thin beams of light emanating from within.

"This looks promising. Deacon, are we there yet?"

Deacon, who has been leading us in silence, finally speaks. "Not quite, but we are in a much nicer place than we were. It's just beyond this mist."

The darkness above our heads starts to clear to a deep purple, progressing to a light lavender as we get closer. The corridor becomes brighter and vines of blue ivy grow on the stone wall, becoming thicker as we walk.

Seth points upward. "Look up."

The arched ceilings of the corridors have opened up, revealing light clouds covering the beautiful lavender sky. I remember the first time I entered the astral plane while under my memory curse last year. The sky was purple in the dimension through the library's portal.

"Look out!" Seth grabs me and moves me to the side. I turn around just as a plant with a conical, fluorescent pink and green flower snaps at my hair.

"Woah, holy shit. What is that?" I lean in to get a closer look. It moves, as if mimicking me. "It's like a snapdragon that really snaps, or a Venus flytrap with a mind of its own." The plant opens its petals to show rows of tiny, sharp teeth. "Oh . . ." I take a step back when it snaps again. "Deacon, I thought you said this place was safe."

"Oh, I never said safe. I said *nicer*, as in, prettier to look at. Come along, we're nearly there."

I walk closer to Seth, watching the plants turn their heads as we walk past them.

"I guess it just wanted to taste you," Seth says. I force a smile and narrow my eyes at him.

The scent of buttercup and gardenia fills my nostrils. My mind floods with memories of my mother working in the garden. Who knew a level in the astral plane could be just as dangerous as the others but also gorgeous? I wonder what the rest of the level looks like beyond the corridor, if this is it, or if we really are just stuck in a labyrinth. I know the reapers have their own special corridors with their own rooms and spaces. I've seen Ambrose's. I move my hand up to the necklace he had given me. I almost forgot I had it. It feels cold in my hands. I really hope that was Ambrose I was with and that he's not dead somewhere. He can't be dead. Reapers don't die.

The vines on the walls grow thicker and are filled with flowers with sweet scents that I have never seen nor smelled before. My stomach grumbles. It's been ages since we've had anything to eat, but I doubt that anything here would be edible. Although, Deacon does know a source for drinkable water, so . . . A rustle in the bushes breaks my concentration.

"What was that?"

"Walk in a single file line right behind me," Deacon orders.

We do as we're told. Another set of leaves ruffle, and I slow my step. My stomach knots.

"Keep up your pace. I'd like to hurry through here," Deacon says.

"What's moving in the bushes?"

"Shh." Deacon moves her finger to her mouth. A green man, fully covered in leaves, with long legs and a tall neck crosses to the other side. My heart nearly leaps from my chest as I come to an abrupt stop. What the fuck is it now? Out to our left, a face entirely camouflaged twists itself out of the bushes and opens his mouth. It has no tongue and no teeth, just blackness like the revitalizer. It moans with a cackling croak. I jolt to catch up with Deacon.

Before I can reach her, one of the snapping plants comes at me, causing me to lose my footing and forcing me to grab onto the bushes next to me. Seth reaches for me, but it's too late.

I fight it off, digging my nails into its branches but its green arms strengthen. Vines grip my legs and pull me into the leaves. I open my mouth to scream and a vine invades my mouth.

"Addison, don't fight it. Just hold still," Deacon says.

A muffled moan comes out as I try to talk. My eyes turn toward Seth. He looks at me helplessly, too afraid to move forward. My chest tightens as I wretch. Tears stream down my face as I gag and resist the urge to vomit. My neck itches from the leaves crawling over it.

Kicking uncontrollably, I manage to look down to see if I can find a stepping-stone, anything to get out of its grasp. But all I can see are bushes. I've become part of the wall.

I'm far past the bitter taste of leaves on my tongue and onto maniacal from basically being put in a plant straight jacket. My lips are cracked and my jaw aches from the branch keeping my mouth open. A sharp pain shoots up my chest. My heart hasn't calmed down since this happened; I'll probably die like this. I've tried kicking and twisting my way out, but the damn vines only get tighter when I do.

My breathing grows raspy. Deacon stands there staring back at me, helpless without her scythe. Isn't there anything a reaper can do without their scythe? Shouldn't she be super strong or something? Besides just standing there like an ornament.

"Hold on, Addison, we'll get you out of there." Seth grips onto the branch in my mouth and pulls it out slowly.

My chest heaves as a few dry coughs escape my throat. I stretch my jaw and lick my chapped lips. "Gross. Deacon! Can't you do something? You don't need to use magick . . ."

"No. I believe you can free yourself." She crosses her arms and I curl my upper lip.

"How? I can't use my magick."

"You have the power to—"

Seth shoots Deacon a look. Her posture stiffens.

A numbness spreads throughout my body. "What are you talking about?"

Seth drops his shoulders and pinches the bridge of his nose.

". . . Seth?"

"This entire time we've been walking, you've believed you were near death. But you have been in less danger than you think." His voice is deep and rigid, like he knows something I don't. But what could he know? And he sure has acted like I've been in danger.

"No, that's not true. I can't use my magick here when I'm in my physical form. Right, Deacon?"

Deacon takes a step back, shaking her head.

Seth steps toward me. "Why do you seek answers from others when you know the answers yourself?" I squint an eye at him as he takes a slow step toward me. "Ask yourself this, Addison: Why do you lack confidence when you carry so much power?"

"So much power? Seth, what are you talking about?"

His eyes darken. Something in him changes.

I try moving, but I've lost all feeling in my legs.

"Kicking won't get you free. You need to search for the darkness within."

"What do you mean? What darkness? Why are you talking in riddles?" What the hell is up with him? Out of all the times, this is the time he chooses to be philosophical.

Seth lets out a long-winded sigh. "This isn't how this was supposed to go."

Leaves rustle and a dark cloaked figure steps out from behind Seth. My heart skips two beats and I try to calm my nerves. A familiar lock of red hair beneath the hood comes into view and my forehead creases.

"Deacon?" Wait–How–Huh? Why are there two Deacons?

"Imposter!" The new Deacon takes out a double-edged ax, similar to the one the guards carry.

"Who the hell are you?" I call out to the new Deacon, not knowing what to think. She turns her head to face me.

"Addison, It's me. I'm the real Deacon. That imposter that's been guiding you is Azazel."

I gasp. No. No, she's lying. The image of Ambrose turning into Azazel flashes in my mind again. *Shit.* I gape at the Deacon who had been guiding me and Seth this whole time . . . Seriously?

"Addison, you can do this. You can get yourself out of there and help me defeat this imposter," Seth shouts at me.

"I can't. I don't know how."

The new Deacon runs toward the other one and swings her ax, chopping the skeleton's head off with one clean blow.

My mouth drops open.

"That's not Azazel, you idiot," Seth says. Now my eyes snap back to him. What did he just say?

He stretches his arm and a dark energy moves toward Deacon.

". . . S–Seth?"

Deacon lifts off the ground. Her eyes grow black and purple veins appear under her skin.

What the hell is going on? "Stop it," I cry. "What are you doing?" How is he doing this?

With a flip of his hand, Seth opens a portal and flings Deacon through it.

My blood drains from my face. The imposter that had pretended to be Deacon reanimates and stands back up, her form now changing. Her face grows a snout, and her skin turns a deep brown, eyes lit red. Tall pointy ears protrude from her head.

I move my eyes from Seth to the imposter. "What the hell is going on?"

Seth shakes his head slowly, looking toward the ground. Without looking up, he snaps his fingers.

Sunshine floods through the window of my small Miami apartment, waking me from my sleep. Taking off my comforter, I stretch, forcing myself to start the day. My legs are heavy as if I slept for a hundred years.

I rub my eyes over the kitchen counter while I wait for the coffee to brew. Turning my head toward the window. I notice the sky is purple and the usually busy street is empty. Just when I'm about to reach for my coffee cup, the front door opens, and heavy footsteps make their way toward me.

"Hey baby," Seth says, handing me a bouquet of red roses.

I take them from him and stand on my toes to give him a kiss. He wraps his arms around my waist as my lips touch his. His warm sandalwood scent engulfs my senses and a similar memory sweeps over me, but I can't pin what it is, a sense of déjà vu.

"You okay, hun?" he asks.

"I think so, just felt strange for a second. Want some coffee?"

"No, I don't drink coffee, remember? I thought we

could have some alone time together." He moves in closer to me, pressing his leg against mine. His eyes are fierce as he stares into me. I see my own reflection in his pupils and move back. Since when does he not like coffee? Memories fire through my mind as I try to remember a time and place where we enjoyed coffee together. I draw a blank. An image of me enjoying my favorite Cuban brew while sitting and laughing with someone I love nearly surfaces to the top of my mind. Seth turns the stove off, putting his hand on my lower back, motioning for me to look out the window. My memories fade.

"What are you doing?"

Seth smiles. "You don't need coffee. Look how beautiful it is today." Not a single bird flies through the sky. A slight breeze rustles the leaves on the trees. I close my eyes as Seth gently strokes my hair.

"So, what do you say we spend the day indoors? Just you and me?"

"Yeah, that sounds nice." I enjoy the relaxing sensation of his nails on my back. The smell of coffee still lingers in the air. "Why don't you go run us a bath? I'll join you in a minute."

He squints at me and then smiles before leaning down to kiss my forehead. I wait as he walks out of the kitchen. Something still feels weird. How could I forget that he doesn't like coffee? Much worse, *my* coffee? I pour some into my mug and take a sip. I spit it out. Yuck! That's bitter. How could I forget to mix the sugar? That's not like me at all. As I move to throw the coffee down the sink, a face shoots through my memories. My head pulses as I try to put a name to this man with light hair and crystal blue eyes. Another image comes. We're drinking coffee in a mansion. This isn't right.

I watch myself kiss the mysterious man, my stomach

twisting itself into knots. Who is he? How can I have feelings for this man if I don't know him? Another shock of pain hits my temple, and I see myself being sucked through a wall and into a garden. There, I see Seth. An evil grin spreads across his face. I collapse to the ground and try to steady myself as the room spins.

"Addie?" Seth calls out over the sound of running water filling the tub. I take two deep breaths and pick myself up off the floor. I spin around, my kitchen coming back into focus. The purple light seeps in through the window and catches my attention again. *Purple.*

"Addie? What's going on? I thought you were coming." His footsteps grow louder as he approaches the hall. My pulse quickens. I have to get out of here.

I open the kitchen door and peer out into the hall. To my left is the front door. I grab the knob and twist it, sneaking out. I don't know where I'll go. All I know is I need to get away from Seth.

The door slams behind me and I turn. A light flicks on to show an old stairway. A scorpion runs across the room, sending prickles down my spine. I'm in an elaborately decorated foyer. A familiar scent of mahogany wafts through the air, causing another shock of pain in my head. I scan the room; I know this place. It's Paradise House. I'm home. Memories flood through my mind. Yes! I remember now. I live here with my father. I have a boyfriend, and he *is not* Seth.

As I look around. Something tells me the house is not the same as when I left it. Slowly turning toward the arched entryway, I tiptoe toward the stairs. I grip the iron stair rail tightly as I climb each terracotta step, trying to look over the opening to the next floor.

Laughter startles me as a child runs past me down the stairs. Here we go again. I get to the top of the stairs and eye the library doors. Hopefully, the portal in there is the right way out of whatever this is. I'm not going to bother with finding my father, or Dax. They'd most likely not be real anyway. The chandelier is dim, giving the place an eerie ambiance.

When I reach the top of the stairs, movement coming out of the kitchen catches my eye. I dare not look. Instead, I book it toward the library door. Prying my fingers through the narrow gaps of the sliding doors, I attempt to pull it apart and panic. It's locked. Of course, it is! My heart races as I scour the table next to me, where the key is normally kept.

The lights shut off and I'm in total darkness. I turn, my back now against the library double doors when a gust of wind blows from the top floor. The firepit bursts into flames and I come face to face with the scorpion demon, Ozo.

My brain tells me to get the hell out of dodge while my feet still don't get the message. I'm frozen like a deer caught in the headlights as the scorpion demon that had cursed my father raises his pincer and aims it right at me.

"Now that you are here, in front of me, you are not getting away," he hisses. "You may think you defeated me once, but now you'll be the one I keep. Yesss, I will feed on you."

I spot an old envelope opener, shaped like a knife on the table beside the library doors, and I reach for it.

I don't know how it got back in my house, nor how the hell I ended up back in this nightmare, but this son of a bitch is about to get stabbed.

"Enough," a voice comes from behind me. Afraid to crane my neck and take my eyes off my assailant, I recognize that the voice belongs to Seth. He approaches from the stairs, and I flick my eye for a second in his direction, my fingers clutching the hilt of the letter opener. Ozo lowers his tail and backs away. My lips part as the scorpion demon retreats like a scolded puppy.

Seth approaches me casually. "Addison, use your skills to kill him."

I narrow my eyes at him. What the hell is he talking about?

"You know how. It's inside of you. Look at him."

Confused, I look back at the gross hairy pincers, and its flat face with its teeth still bared.

"Now is perfect timing, Addison. I have frozen him. Do it now."

"How are you doing this?" I draw my eyes together. The weird illusion I was just in, a fake Deacon turning into a dog-like demon. Seth . . . Has powers? I was being screwed with this whole time!

"What? All this?" He twirls his hand in the air. "This is all you, actually. I took us to the apartment, but us being here in this mansion"—his dimple presses on his right cheek as he steps forward—"is all your doing."

"No . . . That's impossible."

"Oh, it's quite possible. And frankly proves that you're strong enough to lift yourself from an illusion." My mouth dries. Seth was behind all of this? Is he trying to kill me?

"I'm so confused." My voice is in a whisper. "Why . . ."

"Because I want you to use your power," he says as he walks closer. When he inches close enough, I round up my courage and plunge the envelope opener into Seth's chest. Not being sharp enough to protrude easily, I jab it in deeper a second time. I expect him to at least flinch, but he makes no move to stop me. He grabs my wrist and takes the knife, tossing it on the floor. His jaw is stern, but his eyes are filled with grief.

"Addison . . . you would hurt me?"

"Who the hell are you? How are you doing all this?"

"You mean to tell me that after all this time, you would rather kill me instead of this monster standing right in front of you? That really hurts me, Addison." He snaps his fingers and remobilizes Ozo.

"What do you want?"

"For now, just for you to use your power. Turn to face him, Addison."

I look at Ozo, who is raising his pincer once more. "I can't. Not here. Not in the astral. Not in my physical body."

"Trust me, Addison. You can."

"How can I trust you?" Before he can answer, creatures start emerging from the walls, their gaping mouths letting out screeching cries. "Why are you doing this?"

"I'm not, Addison. You are. We are in your corner of the mental plane now."

"Why should I believe anything you tell me?"

"Because I believe in you. And even though you don't think it now, I care about you."

I scoff.

A sharp pain strikes my spine as Ozo grabs me with his prickly claw and lifts me high against the wall.

"Now, Addison! Quickly!"

"What am I meant to do?" I scream.

"The same as before. Forget about where you are now."

The last time I tried magick in the astral plane while in my physical body was to escape the blind guard with the ax, and it didn't work. That was hours ago, no, maybe days? I have no way of telling how much time has passed. I close my eyes and focus on the white ball of energy I used to save my life before. Magick is meant to be raw here, for entities and the astral self. Not for humans.

Ozo squeezes tighter.

My face grows pale as air escapes my lungs. How incredibly stupid was I to go through that portal like this? I had trusted Deacon, that's why. The imposter Deacon . . . The real Deacon was knocked out and sent through a portal by . . . I drop my gaze to Seth and the creatures that are circling the room behind him as if waiting for his instruction. He betrayed me. Anger courses through my veins and into my palms.

"You created him, you know?"

"What?" My concentration breaks yet my palms stay heating up. "Created *what*?"

"Ozo. Well, technically, I gave him life, but you created him out of your nightmares. He's not a natural born demon, this one."

What the actual hell is he on about? "Ozo was not an egregore. He cursed my father . . . and me."

Seth shakes his head. "From my power. That's what happens to an egregore born out of nightmares and then given actual life. He just wants to feed off memories."

I screw up my face. "That makes no sense."

"The monster you were afraid of as a kid. The one your mind made up. I took that egregore and gave it life, just so you could grow up and destroy it."

"Why the hell would you do that?"

Seth chuckles. "So that you could master your power and give yourself strength, of course. You should be thanking me."

"Oh yeah, thanks!" Thanks for nothing, creep. I do remember being a child in the house, afraid to walk out of my room in the middle of the night to get a glass of water . . . I was afraid to step on a scorpion . . . or the dark entity that might be lurking from my father's conjurings. The creatures start to move, towering over me.

"Time is ticking, Addie. Show me what you can do."

This ass hat's voice is getting on my nerves. Why do I keep finding myself as pawns in fake situations like the marionettes in my mother's doll room? I'm sick of being toyed with.

I stare straight into Ozo's beady eyes and let my emotions flood through me. Black energy emanates from my body, shooting out in all directions. Ozo flies out to the center of the living room and disappears from sight, taking the creatures with him.

I remain suspended against the wall and gasp at the height. How am I doing this? My gaze snaps to Seth.

"Are *you* doing this?"

Seth clasps his hands together and smiles. "I knew you were powerful. Just tell yourself to come down."

I inhale and gently let it out, motioning myself to descend to the floor. To my surprise, my feet set me down gently in front of Seth. The house has become overwhelmingly bright, as if all the lights turned on, and the daylight glared bright through the windows, a light violet.

Narrowing my brows, I stare straight at his insufferable smirk. I used to think he was handsome. Now I can't bear to look at him. "You betrayed my trust."

"And for that, I am truly sorry. But there was no other way. Addison, don't you see the power you have inside of you? You never would have discovered it if not for this very moment."

"You don't know that."

"Well, maybe. But it would have taken true hatred for you to conjure up your full power. And I didn't have the time to wait. Besides, you were already taken before."

My chest tightens and my lower lip trembles. "*Were?*" I choke on my words. "What are you talking about?" I pause, recalling all the events that have happened. I fear I know the answer to this, but I have to hear him say it. I gulp. "Seth . . . are you Azazel?"

Seth crosses his arms and his next words leave his lips like venom. "I am."

He gives himself a little shake and curved horns with gold veins grow from his head. His dimples remain the same. I can see the similarities in his features now, yet beside his horns nothing else has changed. How did I not recognize him before? I still cannot believe I'm staring at the demon I met when I first got to LLAPS. "Just a little glamour I use to make people think they're seeing two different forms."

"W–what? But . . ." My eyes drop to the tile floor. Hold up—this can't be right. "How were you in two places at once then? When I first got here . . ."

"Oh, that? Just a smoke screen until I left your side and merged forms. I wasn't really there with my horse. I'm a master illusionist, Addison. You wouldn't have known I was the same person with my glamour on."

My heart launches to my throat. No, this can't be. Not again. Just like Carl, but different. This time it's worse. "I am so sick and tired of people fucking with my memory and my perception of reality." I squeeze my eyes shut, blocking out the vision of Ambrose changing to Azazel. Oh my god . . . And the nakedness. I raise my hand up to my lips and my nostrils flare. I take a deep breath and open my eyes. Peering deep into his I ask: "Us falling into that tight space, being naked together . . . you did that on purpose?"

"Ah, no. In my defense, I did not plan for that to happen. I wanted to get out of that area of the mental plane as quickly as you did, more so even because I knew of the dangers." Fine. But still—

"Did you trick me into having sex with you?"

He raises his chin, his lip curling upward, and I stifle a choked gasp.

"That was you the whole time, wasn't it? Ambrose was never there . . ." My voice trails at the last word.

He nods once and I want to rip his throat out. I back up and grab at my hair. The room spins around me, and I nearly fall to the ground. We had sex! I–I thought he was Ambrose! "No . . ." I clutch at my stomach, pursing my lips together. I feel so violated. I want to puke again.

"Oh, come on. You know me, Addison. It's not so bad."

My mouth gapes open. "You're insane! If you weren't a demon, I would rip your guts out through your nose!" I spit at his face. I did not give him permission . . . I want to run, but I can't. How would I even get out of here? And what about Ambrose? The real one. "Is Ambrose even in LLAPS?"

He smirks and shrugs his shoulders.

"Is Ambrose dead?"

"As I said before, he is gone."

"You said gone to wherever he landed. Did you kill him?"

"How bad would it be if I did?"

It takes everything in me to get close to this man, as disgusted as I am, as much as I hate him. But I collect myself and do so, my nose almost brushing against his chin. "If you killed my boyfriend, I *will* kill you."

Azazel's gaze flicks up, much to my annoyance. "So headstrong. So much anger. This is what I love about you the most. You know what you want."

"So, this whole time, you've been lying to me?" I say between my teeth, my breath shallow. The person I thought was my friend, Seth, tricked me into having sex with him. I still can't wrap my mind around this. "You've been lying to me for the past four months? I don't understand . . ."

"Not about everything. I told you my deepest secrets. I told you about my feelings."

"Why did you do this?"

Azazel moves in closer, forcing me to take a step back. His eyes soften as he places his hands on my shoulders. "Because I love you, and I wanted to show you how good we could be together. Now you know we can be because it was really me the whole time."

I jerk away from him. "You've been stalking me. You left that note in my room. Ambrose has been on to you for a while." I shudder . . . now this makes sense. He just wanted him and my brother out of the way to get to me. "So, this wasn't just for the dagger."

"It started off that way. But then I got to know you and realized it was fated for us to be together. We should get going."

"No, you're crazy, and I'm not going anywhere with you . . . And what do you know about love? You don't even understand why I'm upset with you after you deceived me so savagely!"

His forehead crinkles as he parts his lips. "Addison—" He stops himself. "We have different rules here. I was merely showing you that we work together."

"That is not how you get me to like you. I could never be with someone like you."

He tilts his head back. "I shouldn't have deceived you that way. I apologize."

He *apologizes*? My eyes narrow, searching his for any hint of sincerity. Not that it would matter. "Why do you think you love me?"

His eyes smile with a sadness I haven't seen from him and he swallows. "You . . . remind me of someone I loved dearly long ago. She was just like you—headstrong, fierce, a fire burned inside her—and it used to warm me, just like you do to me." He chuckles softly. "And like you, she too cared about humans. But she didn't see the bigger picture and . . ." His voice cracks. "That's what got her killed."

"Who was that? An ex of yours? You know what? I don't even care. Who the hell were we—who the hell was *I* following this whole time in LLAPS then? Clearly that *thing* wasn't the real Deacon!"

"Only but a gimmick of my powers. I disguised one of my minions to mimic the reaper Deacon. Quite good, don't you think?" A dimple appears on his left cheek as he smooths out his voice. I pale. He can puppeteer his minions to look and act like other people?

Blood rushes to my face. I don't even know how to deal with this. "I hate you."

He sighs, swallows, then looks down and up again. "You can't go anywhere here without me, Addison. You'll never make it out alive."

This is why he was never affected by the revitalizers. My eyes spring up. The crying baby . . . "Wait—that crying demon baby . . . That was your egregore, wasn't it?" My mouth hangs open. "Oh my god, was that you as a baby?" The way they treated him . . . growing up being tortured . . . I shake my head. His forehead wrinkles and gives a subtle nod. I'll take that as a yes. Don't get distracted. He was calling the shots the entire time. This whole time he has just been using me.

"Think I'll take my chances. And in case you haven't figured it out yet. Deal's off. No Ambrose, no deal."

"I didn't say no Ambrose."

"Where is he?"

"You still have to unlock the doors. And then I'll return him to you . . . If you must have him."

"I still don't understand. Why me? It's my dagger."

He clears his throat. "Again, *my* dagger. Your father did not have the dagger made for you. It was entrusted to your lineage by me. The reapers tampered with it to keep me from being able to use it, but what the Judge didn't know was I knew that one day, a half-demon half-angel would be born. I forged that dagger with my own blood to entrust you were the key to be able to use it."

"The blood of a demon?" I gasp. "So, my dagger—"

"It's a special type of key."

"That can open portals."

"It can, yes, but it's much more than that. The night you awakened from your curse; you used the dagger to conjure Paimon. Who, by the way, works for me."

I pause for a moment to think. My father summoned Paimon to bring my brother back from the dead . . . Then Ozo got through . . . sent by Azazel. "You son of a bitch! Why? Why give the dagger to me?"

"Because I needed to hide it with someone powerful. Someone born of LLAPS, someone whose soul is demonic and would one day be strong enough to rule."

My face blanks. "You mean . . ."

"Yes, you."

"But . . . I don't have demon blood." I let my statement linger in the air, but Azazel remains quiet.

"But, how can I?"

"Dark magick flows through your father's veins . . . and yours. It just needed to be awakened."

My head spins. Behind Azazel, a little girl with wavy brown hair places ceremonial items and a piece of old metal on a tray before taking it over to the library podium, where her father waits inside. That's me! Outside, the sun is setting, and the lights on the overhead chandelier dim. Azazel motions for me to watch the scene. I follow my young self to the library. My father, dressed in a long robe, fills up a goblet with mead and flips open his Book of Shadows.

"You weren't raised in an average household, were you?"

"My father wouldn't let me get hurt. He knew what I could handle and what I couldn't."

Azazel shoots me a look from the corner of his eyes. "I agree. So, do you remember what happens next here?"

I nod and watch as my younger self and my father begin the ritual. "This was the first time I was able to channel my powers through and out of the dagger."

"Shhh . . . let's watch."

"What is it that you want, *mi amor*?" Orlando asks.

"I want to be powerful, like you."

A smile spreads across his face. "Then hold the dagger out in front of you and face the fire in the cauldron. Repeat the words, 'I AM powerful.'"

I watch as my young self does as she's told.

"Good," Orlando continues. "Now imagine yourself changing that stone into gold." The little girl closes her eyes, and moments later, the metal starts to shake.

"What's the point of this? We both know it doesn't really happen," I say.

"Keep watching."

The stone levitates above the altar, and little Addison opens her mouth in amazement. Then the stone falls hard, and she frowns as the stone looked exactly the same. Orlando laughs. "You did very well, *mi amor*."

"But it stayed the same. I didn't turn it into gold."

"Did you see it as gold in your mind?"

"Yes, as clear as day!"

"That's why it lifted up in the air. If it worked in your mind, and in your heart, then you have the power to transform your power to greatness. Turning base metals into gold is merely a metaphor. It won't really happen."

The scene before us grows hazy and I step away from the library. "Why show me this?"

Azazel steps back out into the living room. "I didn't. Your mind brings in the memories it wants you to see here."

Mental plane, right. "But why this one? What was so important about that night?"

"For starters, your mind is showing you what you need to get out of here. And secondly, it's the reason why I need you."

I curl my lips at him and shrug. "None of this makes any sense."

"What is alchemy?"

"What?"

"What you were doing in there, that was called alchemy. What did you learn that day?"

"What's this got to do with anything?"

"Everything. Just amuse me."

I sigh. "I learned that turning base metals into gold is a symbol for mind transformation. That I could control and transform my mind."

"Transform it to what?"

Fucking hell, somebody get me out of here! "To the best version of myself."

"Which is what?"

I throw my arms in the air. "I don't know! My father was teaching me to cast and control my magick. What's your point? And what's this got to do with my dagger?"

"Addison, I left that dagger in your possession before you were born, because you are half-demon and half-light. The best version of yourself is to use the dagger for what it's meant for. This whole time, I've been trying to get you to use your other half."

"But why? My other half? I still don't understand. I can't be half-demon, I just can't." I'm panting now. I want to get out here, away from this creep, but if I leave now, how will I find Ambrose? And if Azazel is lying again?

"In order for you to use the dagger, you have to find balance within."

"Why steal it then? Why hide in plain sight this whole time? Why not just tell me the truth from the beginning?"

He sighs.

"And why would a demon also need light magick?"

"With dark magick, alone the dagger can do nearly anything, even control some demons. I had to be careful it didn't fall into the wrong hands. But with light magick, its true purpose is unlocked."

I stare unblinking as my stomach turns to knots. This whole time I was guarding the dagger and didn't even know it?

"I lied to you, Addison, because I wanted you to get to know me for who I am inside. If I had told you the truth from the beginning, you never would have listened to me, and everyone would have tried to cast me out immediately because of who I am. I don't have the best reputation, you know."

I guess the demon Azazel couldn't exactly knock on my door. I raise my eyes to him. "What will happen if I open that door? What will your father do?" I can't believe I'm even asking this question. He's the devil. What wouldn't he do if unleashed onto the world?

"What he's always wanted to do: Change the way magick works in this world. Addison, we both need it to get what we want."

"How will he change magick in this world?"

"There's a lot I want to teach you. A lot you must learn. But for now, know that with this dagger, used by you only, we are levelling the playing field. Imagine the magickal potential opened on the physical plane, coming directly from the astral. Laws of physics broken, and anyone who wants to learn the craft will have the power of the universe to assist them. You can bring your brother back to life, Addison, for real. Not just as a reaper. You and I can both rule the astral levels together. All of them, not just LLAPS."

I scoff. "You really are crazy." Even though I don't want to listen to him, I can't help the way my heart sinks at the mention of bringing my brother back. Would it really be that simple? I imagine him coming back home to live with us, everything as it used to be. Maybe even my mother too.

"Immortality for you and your family."

That would be nice. I shake my head. "What about the reapers? They keep the balance."

"Leave the reapers to me."

"If I do this, I can find my brother and bring Ambrose back."

Azazel frowns. "If you must."

"Tell me what I need to do."

He grins, showing his dimples. "Use the darkness within you."

TRANSPERSONAL ALCHEMY

ADDISON

"So, how do I raise *the darkness within me?*" Still standing in my own living room, or my perception of it, I fight my urge to run and try to keep a cool head. Seth's—or Azazel's— demeanor has changed. He's calculating, calm, and collected. I need to be the same. Despite him fully aware of the fact that I'm stuck, I need to try to fool him into thinking I am not intimidated by him. Even though it's a lie. "And when can we leave?"

"I thought you'd never ask," Azazel says, eyes narrowing on me, reading my reactions. "You've always had it inside you. It's been hidden because of your self-created moral laws."

I resist the urge to roll my eyes but scoff instead. *"Self-created moral laws?"*

"What gives humans the right to decide right from wrong? You are who you are. You should be who you're meant to be."

I arch my eyebrows as he puts his hand out, showing his palms. "No, don't get me wrong. I'm by no means saying that people should get away with murder, but I don't agree with the idea of eternal punishment."

"You don't agree with punishment? What are you talking about? What does this have to do with anything?"

"Everything. This is the whole point of my charade."

"The dagger being the key, you mean?" I say, crossing my arms. "How does opening the veil and uniting the worlds have anything to do with punishment?"

"You ask a lot of questions all at once. One thing at a time." Azazel raises his chin; a thin smile spreads on his lips.

I keep my breathing steady, but I can't help but grind my teeth. I obviously don't trust him, but I need answers. If he created the dagger with all this power, maybe I can use it to kill him. "Where's my dagger?"

"You don't need it yet."

"How am I meant to use it the way I need to if I don't practice?"

"I will tell you this: lawmakers who were put in charge of LLAPS and all the realms took it upon themselves to lock up and punish people who fell victim to the system. I intend on changing that system."

As Azazel speaks, darkness seeps across the room, swallowing the walls, doors, and chandeliers.

"What's happening?" I ask.

"Look." Azazel points to a small window with iron bars that appear on the wall. I walk to it and peer inside. A man with both his arms chained to the wall screams his head off as if he's being tortured. Except, there is no one else in the room with him.

"What's going on? Why is he chained up?"

"We are in the dungeons of LLAPS. Here, there is nothing but floors and floors of cells with people chained to the walls. Enochian sigils keep them in a hypnotic state. Their souls suffer horrendous pain for eternity."

I grimace, turning away.

"Watch," he says forcefully, putting his hand on my shoulder. The scene changes again, and we're in a bedroom. A woman and a man lay in the bed together, kissing passionately. I jump, letting out a scream as a man barges in and pulls the trigger twice. Both man and woman are killed instantly and blood puddles the sheets. I grow pale in the face. Taking a closer look at the man holding the gun, he's the same one I saw in the cell moments earlier. He turns the pistol on himself, pulling the trigger once more. The blast going off makes me squeal and I cup my mouth. Seconds later, a little boy walks into the bedroom and finds them all dead.

Azazel snaps his fingers and we're back in the corridor.

"That was horrible," I say, clutching at my chest. "That little boy . . ."

"That man experiences that scene over and over and over in his mind. But this is nothing, Addison. We've had a limitless amount of prisoners here since the beginning of time. I chose this one to show you because it's modern enough for you to understand."

I nod once and keep my eyes on the prisoner. "So, this *is* hell?" I say more to myself than asking him. I sort of knew the answer already but wasn't sure about where the spectrum of hell falls under LLAPS.

Azazel winces. "I hate that name. This is my home, and it doesn't have to be hell, or at least not in the way you think."

"But that's what it is."

"This is LLAPS. We have prisons, just like on Earth."

"I guess I expected hell to look . . . different."

His eyes darken and his voice lowers to a deadly hiss. "Please stop calling it that."

My breath grows shallow, but I force myself to keep my wits. Straightening myself up, I look him in the eye. "Fine, what I mean is, I expected it to look more fiery, with people carrying large boulders up mountains, with chains hooked onto their ankles. That sort of thing." Although, those egregores with the demons running under a boulder instead of sufficiently carrying them was close enough.

Azazel snaps his fingers again.

I stumble forward, disoriented from the change and snorting up dust, making my nose twitch and sneeze. I wipe my face to see dark gray marks on my hands. Ashes. Something crunches beneath my feet as I step forward. I lift my leg up at the crackle of bones snapping underfoot as if they were branches or twigs. More bones appear throughout the corridor floors and coming from the walls and ceilings as I follow Azazel into the next room. This is revolting. We're going waist-deep in human remains. "Oh, gross." I muffle my words as I hold my hand up to my nose to keep me from gagging.

"What is this?"

Azazel motions for me to come forward. A man is drowning in a room of skulls, his head barely visible as he attempts to save himself. The moment he gets high enough, he loses his footing and falls deeper again.

I want to reach out and help him but know I can't.

I lean next to the border of the door and something pinches my arm. I rub it and squint to see what the hell is piercing my skin. My stomach turns as decaying teeth stick out of the door. I avert my face, toward Azazel, as the stench fills my lungs and my eyes water. "Get me out of here, now."

"Don't you want to know why he's being punished?"

I shake my head violently. Vomit rises up to my throat, but I swallow it down.

"This one's fairly new. A soldier who was taking orders, or so he says." Azazel gives me a sly smile.

Struggling to open my mouth, I talk into my hand. "What side was he on?" is the only thing I manage to get out.

Azazel raises an eyebrow. "Does it matter?"

I nod.

"He died when he threw himself in front of women and children, to save them from death."

"He sounds like a war hero."

"Maybe, but not according to him. In doing so, he left his rank alone. They blew up while trying to reach him. He's here because he feels guilty."

My eyes narrow. "You're not showing me the bad ones. Why?"

Once again, Azazel snaps his fingers and everything around us changes.

The air becomes icy and I wrap my cloak tighter around me. "It got cold so fast . . ."

"That's your ingrained perception of what the temperature should be. Hot or cold are human experiences."

"It can't be. I didn't know where you were taking us."

"That doesn't matter. Your subconscious knows. You still do not understand how in control you are here. If your subconscious believes it is cold, then you will feel cold. There is no absence of energy for your body to react to like on Earth. This is the astral plane. And it is all connected. Your mind determines where you are."

"Oh, so I can just leave if I want to?"

"Technically yes, but it wouldn't change anything."

I jolt at Azazel's touch as he tries to wrap his arms around me, presumably to keep me warm. "Don't touch me," I spit, taking a step forward, causing me to fall an inch, my foot no longer touching the ground. Ohh shit . . . We're floating. I yelp and he gently places his finger on his lips, hushing me.

"Be still."

Spirit-like heads float all around us, shrieking in pain, their eyes hollow. My heart begins to ache as if everyone I have ever known and loved are gone. My throat dries up and I begin to feel a sense of dread.

"The souls in this room committed suicide. They felt unwanted and lost when they were alive, and now they remain in that state."

"Why just their heads?"

"There's no need for them to have bodies. They were so consumed by sadness that it overtook their mind and they let their bodies go."

A head howls as it floats past, its mouth hanging open, emanating sorrow and despair. My head sinks to my neck, my arms tight around me, hating the fact that Azazel still has his arms wrapped around my torso. "I don't want to be here."

"One more stop." Azazel looks up and when the scene changes again, he lets me go. "You said you wanted to see fire."

I turn away from him and lean over a rock wall. On the bottom is an endless fire pit, molten lava falling from the edges and down to the core. Fire shoots up from the middle, roaring as it blasts high. Above, winged men, with tentacles drooping down from where their jaws should be, sit perched like gargoyles. Their menacing yellow eyes follow every move the imprisoned souls make. Men, women, and children in rags carry molten rocks in their bare hands. Blisters that ooze and bleed cover their entire bodies. A woman tosses a rock into the flames, goes back down to pick another, and makes the same journey back to the fire pit.

"What are they doing?" I ask.

"Those who spent their lives in greed, fixated by their material possessions while ignoring those in need around them, are now stuck in an endless and meaningless task. Making the pit larger, only to do it again and again."

"Why are there children down there?"

"Sometimes when people die, they return to the state they imagine themselves as. Some may look like children when they're not, while others died as greedy kids."

I gape at him and snap my jaw shut. "That can't be fair."

He smiles. "This is exactly what I am trying to correct."

"Right, but how? What about the ones who have committed rape, murder? What about the pedophiles?"

"Some are better off being disintegrated, which isn't even an option at the moment. But we can make it so that energy gets recycled as something different, other than a spirit. But for the rest, what about rehabilitation?"

Not sure recycled spirit energy is better than torture for pedophiles in my book. "What about it?"

"Don't you see? The reason why there are so many endless variants of punishment is because they created it themselves. Remember I told you that down here your subconscious manifests what you see and experience. People have preconceived notions of what this place should be and should look like, so they create their own hell."

"I thought you said the lawmakers put them here. So, you're just gonna let sinners, killers, rapists roam free?"

"No, I only want to remove their mental chains. If they ascend, they've overcome their egos, their cruel nature that put them here. They put *themselves* here, not my father, not me, not any god. Them."

"And the lawmakers?"

"They are in charge of who comes down, but what they experience when they get here is up to the prisoners. This fire pit is for the people who envisioned this version of hell. The rest get trapped in their own personal despair, whatever it might be. The only way for them to learn and be rehabilitated is for—"

"Them to rise above it."

"Precisely."

Shadows from the flames dance on his face. The corner of his lips curls and a twinkle shines in his eye as he gazes at me.

I flick a glance over my shoulder at the people moving burning rocks around for no real purpose. A man bends down to grab a rock that is clearly too heavy for him, causing him to topple backward and trip over his feet. One of the demons sweeps down from a pillar and breathes out a stream of fire. The man catches in flames and falls into the pit, screaming and flailing. Minutes later, he climbs out of the pit, skin hanging from his body, to start his task again.

Off to the side of the pit, a lonely burned one, with flesh falling off its face, climbs out and floats away in the opposite direction. Another one follows, leaving behind a trail of ash as it hovers. "The burned creatures from earlier . . . This is where they come from?" My eyes follow them as they disappear into the inky blackness of the abyss behind us.

"Yes. After so many centuries of doing the same thing, some of them—but very few—manage to make the decision to go the opposite way. They wander the corridors until they are found and sent back to the pit."

"So, the guards don't actually kill them?"

"No, they rise from the pit."

"What's the point of that?"

"They cannot rise above. Simply put, the lawmakers won't allow it."

I shake my head and scoff. "What about people throughout history who've committed heinous crimes?"

"Like who?"

"Hitler, for example. He doesn't deserve to rise above his actions."

"Says who?"

My mouth gapes open. "But he killed millions of Jews! He was a disgusting racist. He should be burning here for all eternity, surely!"

"Oh, he is. But everyone should be able to learn and rise above their own punishment."

"I'm not sure I believe that everyone is capable of redeeming themselves."

"You will," Azazel says smugly. Fat chance at that, buddy. "Or we disintegrate the racist. Start over, your choice. Are you ready?" Without waiting for a reply, he snaps his fingers and the lava around us grows dark and cold. "Do you believe in the death penalty, Addison?"

"Not really, but well, I suppose it depends on the case."

"But you *do* believe in eternal punishment?"

I grow quiet. Honestly? He got me there. "I guess it's just not up to us to decide."

"Right, so the Judge knows better. He pretends there's an order he follows, when he's the one who set forth all these rules. Can you imagine what eternity feels like? You cannot destroy a spirit, Addison. Only transfer it to take a different shape."

"I know that, it's energy." Wait, is the Judge like, *God?* He interrupts my thought before I can ask.

"Correct. Don't you think it's a waste of a spirit, a waste of energy to keep them all imprisoned, with no way out? No way to learn from their mistakes, no matter how heinous?"

"But where would they go? Heaven?" I say, searching his face.

Azazel scoffs. "No such place. The will is your own. Where do you want to go? Heaven? So, create it. I don't care. But to just accept torture for all eternity, even in the face of full repentance, is unknowingly cruel. And quite frankly, unimaginative. Boring. Why be stuck in a so-called hell created by a so-called forgiving god?"

I sigh. "Perhaps, but it's a good thing I'm not the one making these decisions. Where's 'god' in all this? Are you implying that the Judge is . . .?"

"No. But he took it upon himself to take on that role. And as a matter of fact, Addison, I'm hoping that you will partake in making decisions."

Before I can register what he just threw at me, a laugh escapes the back of my throat. But there is no amusement in his eyes. "You're serious?"

He nods.

"I'm just a nurse."

His features soften as he measures my expression. "That means you care about people. And the fact that your mother is angelic brings your light up to balance with the demonic blood in your soul. It makes you *perfect.*"

A warm sensation touches my chest. "My mother was an angel?"

"She became one, because of her virtuous life—she always followed the way of the light. Just like your father's affiliation with dark magick seeped into you in the moment of conception."

I drop my gaze, taking in what he just said. How would I make any decisions? "You're asking me to stay here?"

"With your power, you could break the loop. You'll be changing the course of existence; don't you think that's important?"

He really is insane. He didn't only bring me down here to release his dad, he really wants me to rule with him. Like marrying him. I mean, what the fuck? "What if I say no?"

"No?" Azazel raises an eyebrow.

"I have a life. My father, my home, my friends . . ."

"Your father would find it much more comfortable here, once he's immortal. He can even stay in his mansion, or add another wing to it. You can do anything here, Addison. Why would you want to leave?"

"I'll tell you why." Here's my chance to bring it back to finding my boyfriend.

"Go on?"

"Because of Ambrose. If you are so hell-bent on rehabilitation, why did you kill him?"

"I did not kill Ambrose. I sent him away."

My pulse quickens. He's alive? "Where is he? Where did you send him?"

"Addison, it's best for you to forget about him. He was no good for you—for us."

"Why do you keep saying *was*?"

"Ambrose is no longer the man you remember, or the one *he* remembers for that matter," Azazel says with a smirk.

My hands shake as I take one step toward him. "What the hell is that supposed to mean?"

"I wiped his memory. He doesn't even remember you." He clasps his hands together. "Now you know everything. Shall we get a move on?"

Blood drains from my face. "You . . . wiped . . . his . . . memory . . .?"

"That's right. He has no memory of being a reaper, or of you, or of anything."

"You're a monster." I step against the stone wall behind me.

"Oh, come now. Humans have done far worse."

"Bring him back."

"I'm afraid I can't do that."

"Can't . . . or *won't?*"

Azazel smiles. "Won't."

"If you give him back his memory, I'll stay here with you."

"No."

"Why? You want me to be with you that badly? But I don't love you! And I never will! You took Ambrose away from me."

"Because he's a part of the Reaper High Council, that's why," he says, cocking his head back.

"What? What's that got to do with it?"

"Reapers think they can decide the fate of everything!"

I shake my head. "No, no that's not true. Ambrose just guides them; he doesn't decide what happens to them."

Azazel laughs. "Ambrose is a rogue. He isn't a robot like the rest of them. But that Judge started all this. He caused me and my father pain and suffering, and he deserves to be punished."

"You're contradicting yourself. Why punish Ambrose and Deacon and all the other reapers because of one Judge? You're the one claiming everyone has the right to be released from torment. Why are the reapers any different?"

"I have plans for them. But first, they must understand

why they are wrong. And I, *we*, will be the new Judges, the new rulers."

"I still don't understand. Why wipe Ambrose's memory? Did you do that to the rest of them?"

"Because Ambrose is just like the Judge."

"Oh . . ." My eyes sparkle with a thought. "You're afraid he will beat you. Well, my brother is still out there. You told me he is fine, right? He'll figure something out."

Azazel laughs. "Your brother is wherever I need him to be. For now, at least. If you comply."

I choose my next words very carefully. "Fine."

Azazel raises a brow. "Really? Just like that?"

"You said I'm the only one who can do this, and it's the only way I can save my loved ones so . . ."

"I'm glad you see it my way."

"So, where's my dagger?"

A gold door appears in the gray stone. He opens it, and inside is a beautiful gold and red room filled with large cushions, and plates of fruits and chocolate. I spot my dagger high up on a mantel.

"Inside," he says, pointing toward the door.

Taking a deep breath, I walk into the room.

Azazel begins to whisper something, and I spin around to catch him staring at my hands. I flick my eyes down and gasp as two gold cuffs appear on my wrists.

*M*y eyes cut to the Enochian engravings decorated on the cuffs on my wrists and I forget to breathe.

"What did you do?"

"I'm sorry, but I can't take any chances, Addison. This needs to happen. It *is* going to happen, and like I've said before, you're the only one who could take the reins of LLAPS. I can't have you plotting your escape with the dagger in your hands. I wish it could be different."

I bring my eyes to his as heat radiates from my face. To think we had a "moment" in that tight tunnel we fell into. All I want to do now is punch the smugness off of his features. "So, I'm your prisoner now? Why didn't you just do this before then?"

"Well, I tried to make you see it my way."

"But . . . I do understand. I do see it your way!" I yell, panic now tightening in my chest as I realize he does not intend on letting me go, no matter what decision I make. He can hold me here forever. "No more veil separating our worlds. A chance for people to ascend from their torment.

I get it Azazel, I do. But there still needs to be order or there'll be chaos."

"I can handle the chaos."

I shake my head and yank at the cuffs. I'm going to have to try my very best to kill him with my wrists cuffed.

Azazel laughs. "Trust me, there's no way you're getting out of those. You can't leave." My breathing slows and I follow him with my eyes as he walks to the mantle where he keeps my dagger. Taking hold of it, his pupils dilate as the glare from the hilt reflects in his eyes.

"It is beautiful, isn't it? One of the nicest pieces I ever had to create." His eyes grow soft, for a moment distancing himself as he glares at the ruby hilt.

"Had to?"

"You're not the only one who's been a prisoner, Addison." He steps closer to me, twirling the dagger in his hands. "But here it is now, ready to be put to good use. You see, it needed to be forged with my blood. I knew that in order to use it, it needed to be held by a human with equal parts light and dark."

"But why?"

"Because what this key opens was locked for the purpose of light. This magick spans LLAPS, and only a specific mix of power can break it. Power like yours." Azazel spins the dagger in one hand and hands me the hilt. I grab it. The dark ruby hilt glistens as I turn it to its side, remembering the last time I had to use it, to summon Paimon.

"Go on, give it a whirl."

"A whirl?"

"Awaken the darkness within you. Give it your best shot."

My gaze falls back down to the weapon. Here's my chance. Heat spreads to my fingertips as power and fury surges through me. It's now or never, then I can use it to open a portal out of here. Or wherever Ambrose actually is. I raise my cuffed wrists above my head and slam the dagger down hard into Azazel's chest.

I let go of the dagger and take a step back, waiting for Azazel to collapse to the ground.

"What were you thinking?" Azazel's smile fades as he pulls the dagger straight out without flinching. "Did you think you could kill me with this?"

I back away slowly. Oh fuck, fuck, fuck. That didn't work. Can nothing kill this asshole? I was sure that would work!

"Now, why would you want to do that?" He turns the dagger over, handing it back, hilt first. "I made this; it can't kill me, Addison. Stop being a fool and do as you're told."

"I'm sorry, I . . ." Just thought it would be better than a letter opener.

He smiles again. "You don't need practice. You just tried to kill me without a second thought, you little demon you. You're so perfect."

I gasp. I had just attempted to kill him again. I had tried to kill him when I still saw him as my friend, Seth, not once but twice. Even knowing he's a demon, I shouldn't want to hurt him so instinctually, right? My eyes fall back to the dagger . . . maybe there *is* a darkness in me . . .

But it was my only option at the time . . . And now, I don't have another choice in the matter. I can't bear to lose anyone else. I need to go through with unlocking the cage.

"Just tell me how to open it."

"Right through here." Azazel turns and spreads his arms out. A tall black double door with Enochian etchings from top to bottom appears on the wall in front of us.

My eyes follow the scriptures that seem etched into the iron, but the more I look at them, the more I notice them changing, transforming into different scriptures, glistening as they change. What am I meant to do? A voice speaks in my mind, as plain as day.

Open it.

I look over my shoulder back at Azazel. He gives me a nod of encouragement. Who is this?

The one who's going to get you out of here. Now, open it . . .

But how?

Use your will, Addison. Any memory you can muster of you ever being happy or angry, bring it all to the surface at the same time.

I inhale and hold the dagger in both hands, raising it to face the doors. I concentrate hard on happy memories. Envisioning myself being back in Ambrose's arms, both of us safe and sound. Everything going back to the way it was before. Summoning bliss from these thoughts, I'm at ease, a calm so deep within me that I nearly forget I need to remember a time I was angry. Azazel's face appears in my mind's eye, deceiving me the way he did, wiping Ambrose's memory, cuffing me. Anger boils my innards. I grip the hilt of my dagger so tight I start to shake.

Good, now draw those feelings together and open the damn door.

FOLLOW THE AYAHUASCA

DAX

The City of Petra disappears from my line of sight, and I slow Yiri, a camel I rented while talking to the people of Jordan. Deacon told me what the dangers of a reaper becoming human could imply. So, memory loss is something I'm aware of. I take the ayahuasca vine from my pocket. Holding it tight, I whisper, "Lead me to Ambrose."

The vine gives off a green glow and a light shoots out from it, snaking across the desert, forming a path.

I click my tongue. "Onward, Yiri!"

Hang on Ambrose, I'm coming for you. Why Azazel would strip a reaper of his immortality and send him off into the desert is beyond me. Sick sense of humor? Perhaps.

I don't know why Deacon's portal didn't lead me right to where Ambrose is. The only thing I can think of is he's been moving around, or the Enochian sigils Azazel carved on his chest also make it hard to find him.

I swallow at the latter. The high chances this vine could be leading me to his dead body are far too real. I shudder to think . . . No, just keep going. He's strong. He might not understand sarcasm and my jokes may go over his head, but he's a fighter. He's still Ambrose, reaper or not. I *will* bring him home, if it's the last thing I do.

Clouds of dust raise as a strong gust of dry wind, causing the hood of my cloak to smack me right in the face. I let go of the reign to move it back and within seconds the dust has thickened, reducing the minimal light I had from the stars to almost zero. The only thing I see now is the glow from the vine, but just barely. Oh, wonderful. A dust storm? Really? Now?

I reach over to grab hold of the reign just as Yiri head-butts me right in the forehead. Ow! Son of a bitch that hurt!

The light from the vine flickers. I arch a brow. What does that mean? I raise it back up to my lips and shout over the heavy winds increasing in speed. "Find Ambrose!" The vine flickers on and off. Uh oh . . . Is it too small? Not enough power to last? This will be challenging if I'm meant to use it to transport us both back to LLAPS. I could light up my hand like I had in the rainforest, but that's probably a bad idea considering the dry winds.

The man at the internet café where I rented Yiri told me he had seen Ambrose. Apparently, he had gone with a Bedouin man to use the phone and had trouble remembering the phone number. Luckily, I had been paying attention when he pointed me in the right direction of the small Bedouin village two hours from here. I thought the vine would be enough. I tuck it into my pocket. Best not to use it all up. I'll just have to brave the dust storm without its guidance for now. Wherever Ambrose is, I hope he's safe from all this.

Yiri backs away as wind makes zapping sounds out in front of us. I swallow, my lips becoming chapped from the arid region. A dust devil or tornado. Yiri grunts and I nearly fall off the camel as two large eyes emerge from the cloud of dust. Okay, that's not normal.

"Stay calm, Yiri," I say to the camel but more to myself. This isn't just a regular sandstorm. This must be part of Azazel's doing. I'm being watched. The eyes come down at me at lightning speed. I duck, pressing my cheek against Yiri's neck as she cranes it back. I wince, expecting her to snap back and bop me again but she misses. As quick as the eyes come at me, the cyclone of wind it brings with it disperses with the eyes all together. I sit up as the dust settles around me.

Well, that was not a good sign. But one thing's for certain. We're headed in the right direction.

It takes me a couple more hours before I reach a small village. I stop at the top of a hill, looking down and stretching my neck. This must be the Bedouin town the café owner told me about. I see a man in desert robes holding a knife to his throat. I catch a view of his light-skinned hand and know instantly. Ambrose.

"Yiri!" I click my tongue and the camel descends us down the sand dune. Killing yourself isn't the answer, you brute.

"Stop!" I yell. With a shaky hand, the man lowers the knife and turns. "No, you can't, Ambrose. That's not the way."

"W—who are you?"

He really is losing his memory. "I get what you were trying to do there, buddy, but believe me, you don't want to get lost in the astral that way. Especially with what's going on over there at the moment." I park Yiri and jump down.

Ambrose's blank stare makes my gut sink. This must be torture for him.

A woman runs out of the house. "Who are you?" Her eyes are red and puffy as if she's been crying.

"I'm a friend of Ambrose," I say calmly. "I've been looking for him." She must be with the man they had seen him with at the café.

Her eyes well up as they land on Ambrose holding the knife and then back to me. "My husband found him in the desert . . ." Her voice cuts off.

"He's dying." Ambrose finishes for her. "I keep feeling like there's something I need to do. It comes and goes. My memory . . ."

He's feeling the pressure of his duties, no doubt. "I'm here now. You have to come with me." I dig into my pocket for the ayahuasca vine. Hopefully this works.

"No, wait! You can't go. What about my husband?"

"He's dying, you said?" She nods. Two reapers and nothing we can do. It's a long shot, but I have to return my camel anyway. "We'll drop him off at the hospital first." It would be good to give Ambrose a bit of his memory back before heading off.

The woman's eyes light up. "I'm Rahima, please come inside. Help me get him."

Inside of their home, I sit Ambrose on a chair and force feed him a piece of the vine. Getting a toddler to eat would be easier. If I weren't in such a hurry, I'd pretend my hand was a plane and make airplane sounds. Video tape it too while I'm at it. Minutes later, after Ambrose fidgets and fights me before eating the bitter ayahuasca, his pupils dilate and come back to normal.

He screws up his face, stares right at me, and wraps his arm around me.

"Thank you. How did you find me?"

"Anytime. And later. Right now, we have to hurry the hell up out of here." I turn to face Nabil, the man lying in his death bed, purple in the face, and suffering on accounts of there being no reapers to collect him. He won't make it, but anything is better than him being here.

We ride alongside each other, Ambrose with me on top of Yiri and Rahima with her husband on their camel. The trip doesn't take nearly as long as it did through a sandstorm, thankfully. After dropping them off at the nearby hospital, Ambrose and I make back to the internet café where I return Yiri and take a turn into a desolate area where no one can see what we're about to do.

I cut the vine into two pieces, take a bite and stuff the other one into Ambrose's mouth. It takes me forever to convince him to eat the damn thing because the last bit of it holding his memory intact wore off.

I hold onto Ambrose's shoulder to keep him from collapsing. Images of the LLAPS' corridors zip through my mind. This needs to work. I need . . . something to grab on to, to pull us in. But fall short.

I get zapped back to my desert surroundings. No! The morning light bores down on me and sweat drips from my forehead. I dart my gaze to Ambrose, whose features are twisted in a state of confliction and confusion. Oh shit . . . please don't tell me he lost his memory again . . .

"Dax! What happened?" I let out my breath. Good.

"It wasn't enough."

"What do you mean it wasn't enough? How much did you take last time?"

"I'm not sure, but I was able to communicate with Deacon."

Ambrose rubs his cheeks and looks up at the sky. "He saw me."

"Who did?"

"Azazel. He looked right at me when I shouted out Addison's name."

"Wait, you saw Azazel?"

"Yes, didn't you?"

"No, I saw the council headquarters, barren and destroyed. I was looking for something to grab a hold of. I didn't even hear you shouting."

He chafes his chin, looking down at the ground. "That's curious. We mustn't have been looking at the same timeline."

"We were standing right next to each other, looking through at the same time, Ambrose."

"No, smart ass. I mean we weren't looking at the same time frame. Whatever we saw is either happening at the moment or has already happened." I part my lips. Smart ass? I chuckle, glad to know I'm still rubbing off on him.

"How do you know we weren't just looking at two different areas, at the same time?"

He draws his brows together. "Could be, but it doesn't matter anyway. We couldn't get through. So, what now?"

"Dammit," I shout. "That was the last of it." I kick a nearby rock to the side of a red wall. "What the hell do we do now, Ambrose? My sister is with Azazel." And without the vine, or a way to get back . . . If Ambrose loses his memory for good, I'll be all out of options.

"She must have gone looking for us. You know your sister. Also, Azazel most likely tricked her somehow."

"My sister isn't easily tricked." I rub my forehead. Time for a plan B . . . But what?

"Listen to me, Dax . . ." Ambrose's voice is low and somber. "We have bigger problems now. Very soon, I'll be completely human and entirely useless to you." He straightens his back and stares into my eyes. But I shake my head. I don't want to hear this right now. "Listen to me. Whatever happens, I need you to do whatever it takes to save Addison and take Azazel down. Leave me here. I'll only hold you back."

I grab his shoulders. "What? Not gonna happen. I'm not leaving you in the desert alone."

"You don't have a choice. I'll only slow you down. Come back for me once it's over. But for now, you need to do what's right."

"I don't know how I'm going to get there without my scythe."

"I trust you'll find a way, just like you got yourself here to find me. You're clever, Dax. I wouldn't have chosen you as my apprentice if I didn't think you were capable."

I take one long look at him and draw him in for a hug. "Listen to me, I'm going to get you into a hotel first. We'll figure it out then."

He pulls away. "Woah, who are you? What are you talking about? A hotel? For what? What am I doing here?"

Oh, you have got to be kidding me.

A strange sound of spinning vents come from behind Ambrose. Yes! We're saved! Deacon! Please be Deacon! My face pales as a black portal opens and two skeletal figures saunter through. I grin as I catch sight of Deacon's red hair peeking out from beneath the second figure's robe. Then glance up at the Judge's hard eyes and swallow.

Out of all the reapers in LLAPS, this is the least understanding one to deal with Ambrose right now. I exchange a look with Deacon as she shrugs her shoulders apologetically. The Judge's hollow eyes peer into Ambrose's new human soul and I ball my fist. For the first time in history, he's speechless and his silence is freaking me out. What's he going to do? This is the most by-the-book son of a bitch to ever walk creation. He could incinerate Ambrose with a snap of his bony fingers, and that would be the end of it. The end of *his* problems, but we'd be left having to pretend we agree with him.

Deacon approaches Ambrose, who is seated in the shade of the rock wall. She moves his face from side to side in her hand, inspecting his features. "Azazel really did a number on you," she says.

Ambrose twists his face, pulling away from her grasp. "Do I know you?"

"Is there anything you can do, Your Honor?" I ask the Judge, hoping for dear life that he won't be a dick.

The Judge stiffens with an arched brow directed at me.

"It's been centuries since I walked among humans." He turns to Ambrose, who is now sitting, frightened at the sight of the skeleton standing in a long cloak in broad daylight. I stifle a laugh. How much of an asshole would I be if I snapped a photo of the way Ambrose is looking at the Judge right now? It would only be funny if he survives this, so I wouldn't even if I had a camera on me. "I know Ambrose has been romantically involved with your sister, something that's strictly forbidden," the Judge says with emphasis on the word *forbidden*. "As much as I want to stop Azazel, my duty here is to bring you back, Dax. We need you now more than ever—"

Oh hell no. "I'm sorry, I mean no disrespect, Your Honor, but are you thinking of leaving Ambrose here, alone? In his current state?"

"He broke our laws and got himself into this mess. He's human now, and there's not much I can do. We can't take him back with us."

"If I may," Deacon cuts in. "We can at least try to recover enough of his memory so that he remembers who he was and remembers Addison. I know you're not a fan of his disrespect for our laws, but it is cruel to just leave him here."

"What about the Akashic waters?" I ask.

The Judge chafes his jawline. He takes out his scythe from the inside of his cloak. "The Akashic waters will flood him with eternal memories, possibly rendering him in a permanent state of delusion. We don't know what it could do to him. It's not meant for humans. It would have to be done with my scythe and, as Deacon suggested, a limited amount of memory."

I pass a look to Deacon and shrug.

"It, of course, has to be up to him, if he wants it," he says.

Ambrose sits with his head below his knees. He looks up, clears his throat, and stands up. "I know I'm suffering from some kind of amnesia, and I don't know why. But if what you're telling me is true, I'll only get half of my memories back?"

"Less than half," the Judge says.

"But what about my youth? My childhood, those memories?"

Deacon and I look at each other, unsure of what to say.

The Judge moves toward Ambrose and calmly says, "You were a reaper, like me. You did not have a childhood; I am the closest thing to a father you had."

Ambrose continues to back away. "You mean, I–I'm like you?"

"Yes. And if you want to remember, there isn't much time." The Judge crosses his arms. Can't expect his kindness to last more than a minute. But he's right, we're running out of time.

"Ambrose, you're in love with my sister, and you would want to remember her," I say.

The Judge tips his chin down, his frown deepening.

"I know this is a lot for you to take in, but we really need to hurry," Deacon adds.

"Okay." Ambrose steps forward. "What do I need to do?"

The Judge moves in at once, gripping his scythe. It glows a bright blue for a second, flooring Ambrose to his knees. He hits the wall hard and he grabs onto his head, grunting. He sinks down with his head buried between his knees. I inch forward, unsure of what I can do to help.

After a minute of heavy breathing, Ambrose finally calms down. He blinks and focuses on the three of us standing in front of him.

"How far back can you remember?" I say.

Ambrose squints. "I know I was a reaper. And I remember that Addison is in trouble. We have to go!"

"You cannot come," the Judge says, determination in his voice.

"I thought you might say that, but I'm going anyway."

"Ambrose, maybe you should stay here. You're powerless in LLAPS, and who knows what Azazel will do now that you're human? You could die," I add.

"If that happens, I'll figure out how to be a reaper again in LLAPS. I'm not asking, I'm going."

The Judge straightens his back and fixes his jaw. "You keep defying my laws, you think you can do whatever you want. Not this time; I forbid it. Stopping Azazel *is* the priority. He has imprisoned all reapers and is attempting to open the veil, combing the worlds. Keeping your girlfriend alive is the least of my worries, especially as she is the catalyst in all this."

I feel myself grow paler than normal at the mention of my sister. "What do you mean she's the catalyst? She only went because she thought we were in danger. She had been expecting us, and if I know my sister—"

"Silence." The Judge holds up his hand to my face and I grit my teeth. "She has been harboring a special key, disguised as a dagger. Only she can use it to open the astral veil."

"I don't know if harbor is the right term when you—" Deacon gets cut off.

"Silence!"

Deacon shuts up and I arch a pointy brow, my eyes widening. "No, she couldn't have known. How would she have known Azazel?"

"She was tricked. She knew him as a man named Seth. Our mission is to seize the dagger and imprison the prince. I am sorry, Ambrose, but you will only hinder the mission."

"And what about me?" I say. "She's my sister. I'm not going to let her die."

"Your sister made a choice to go into the astral plane in her physical form. Dax, you need to do as I say while we're there."

Fire surges in my core, and I fight to keep my newfound power under wraps. "Or what?" I spit.

The Judge, clearly taken aback by my tone, lowers his voice to a scolding hiss. "Am I going to have to leave you here as well? Now, Deacon. We need to make haste."

I dart a glance at Deacon, hoping she can infer what I believe we have to do. She gives me a stiff nod and I think she's got it. If not, it'll just be me, but fuck it, I'm strong enough. To my surprise, Deacon joins me and together, we rush at the Judge. I pin him to the ground and Deacon grabs his scythe. She opens a portal, and the three of us jump in, taking the Judge in with us.

"SLEPT SO LONG"

ADDISON

A fiery glow seeps through the cracks of the doors. I concentrate on directing my magick through the dagger. The strange voice resonates in my mind again.

You're almost there, come on, open it!

Behind the doors, a rumbling causes the door handles to shake. Heat singes my face as they shake harder. My guess is there's fire on the other side. My ears start to ring, the noise shattering my concentration. I take a few steps back in case these doors swing open and send me crashing backward. Sigils on the door disappear one by one. As symbols vanish one at a time, the hinges rattle, like they're loosening. My heart pounds and I drop my arms a little bit, unsure whether to stop or to keep going.

Don't stop!

I turn back and look at Azazel, who's put some space between us. Eagerness in his eyes, he motions for me to continue with his hand. I hold up my dagger, refocusing my energy. Getting these doors open is the only thing I have left to bring Ambrose back.

"Addison, wait!"

I can't hear my name being called over the noise. The last sigil almost disappears from the center of the doorway, but the banging stops. I lower the dagger and hold my breath.

Open it! Ignore all else!

My hand gets pulled to the side and the cuffs squeeze against my skin. The motion spins me around and I hold out my arms. I jerk back, pulling my wrist from whatever is pulling at my cuff. But then I see his face.

"Ambrose?" I throw my arms around him and hold him close, tears streaming down my face. "I was so worried about you."

"I was too, once I realized you were here and who you were with."

My brother and Deacon, both holding weapons and pointing them toward Azazel, emerge through the passageway I had come in with Azazel. Beside them stands a reaper I don't recognize. Ambrose pulls away and we look into each other's eyes.

"Ambrose, where have you been? I was so worried."

"I was shot out into the desert and stripped of my memories. Addison, I'm human now. If your brother hadn't found me out there, I wouldn't have any memory of who I was at all. The Judge of the Reaper Council"—Ambrose motions toward the other reaper—"did me a favor by helping me regain a small amount of my memories. I came because I knew you were in trouble."

I freeze. Did he just say . . . "Human?" is all I manage to mutter.

Ambrose's face slackens and he nods.

"But how?"

"Azazel can't kill reapers, but he has the power to alter reality. He wanted to keep us apart."

"I know." My nostrils flare. "I was about to . . ." I

slowly turn my gaze to the doors I'd almost unlocked before being interrupted.

Behind Ambrose, Azazel strides toward the Judge, a pair of black wings erupting from his back. Just when I thought I'd seen all of him.

"You," Azazel mutters.

The Judge doesn't cower. He grips his scythe, turning it to a shade of dark blue and swinging it back. Before he can strike, Azazel grips the Judge's arm, turning the blade from blue to red. Deacon yells and charges at him.

"Get out of here!" Dax bellows at me and Ambrose as he lunges toward Azazel. I wince as my brother gets flung across the room by one of his wings. I let out a squeal as he hits the ground.

I let go of my breath when he stands up. "I can't leave." I hold up my wrists, showing them my cuffs. "I'm spellbound."

The Judge gets flung up against a wall, immobilized, and he lets his scythe drop to the ground. It clanks as it hits the stone floor. Azazel approaches him, eyes narrow, his mouth twisting into a menacing sneer.

"Surprised to see me?" His voice is low and hoarse as he inches closer to the Judge. "You've no idea the pain I've endured from your betrayal." The Judge squirms against the wall. "Because of you, I've had to live my life in solitude, left alone to deal with the misshapen world of LLAPS. Because of you, I've been kept from my father. And why? Because of your rules?" Azazel's breath is hard and heavy as he corners the Judge. "Your stupid ideologies. Trapped in *hell* because of you." His voice rasps at the word as he moves in closer. "I'll let you in on a little secret. There were loopholes in all your rules, and I took advantage of them. I waited patiently for the right moment, and here it is."

Muffled words come from the Judge's mouth.

"Oh, what's that? I can't hear you over the sound of *'I'm in charge now!'*"

Dax, who has been silently creeping up behind him, raises his weapon. Azazel flicks his wrist and freezes him to the spot without giving him a glance. Shit, what do we do? I spot Deacon, whose features look occupied, like she's searching for an idea. Or, at least, I hope she is.

"Now, you're going to stay here as my prisoner and watch your rules become undone. You'll watch as I release all the prisoners and unite the planes with Earth. Oh, and you'll watch *him* be released too. That's right. I'm saving you for *him*."

"What do we do?" I whisper.

Azazel turns his attention to us and flicks his wrist. I scream as Ambrose gets flung against the wall, just as he had done to the Judge. Ambrose flinches in pain and lands with a hard thud. He kicks his feet, struggling to move, but Azazel advances on him, a new scythe materializing in his hand.

"Recognize this?"

Ambrose looks down, wincing.

"Beautiful, isn't it? I always take pride in my work. I hope you enjoyed it, because it's mine now. Oh, and so is she." He motions toward me and I grit my teeth.

"No! Let him go. You promised! We had a deal!" I scream.

"Oh, I promised? Don't you still have a job to do?"

I glimpse back at the last Enochian symbol on the door.

"Let's raise the stakes, shall we?" Azazel snaps his fingers and dozens and dozens of demons, wearing black-plated armor over leather and chainmail cowls over their pointed ears, start crawling up from the ground. Dax and Deacon struggle to fight off two of them.

"The ball is in your court now, Addison. Either finish what you started, or watch your brother and lover be devoured by my minions."

Every fiber of my being tenses beyond measure. My eyes dart from my brother to Ambrose. He can't kill the reapers, but what's to stop him from turning Dax into a human and then killing him? I swallow hard as Ambrose jerks, motioning to me. I furrow my brows as he mouths the word *no*, but the rest I can't understand.

I shake my head, pleadingly. I have to. I don't have another choice.

Azazel's ear twitches as he hears the whirring sound of a portal opening, followed by a low rumbling that shakes the walls. Thousands of reapers march into the room, all holding weapons previously belonging to the guardsmen of the corridors. I glance at Deacon, who has her hand on the Judge's fallen scythe, despite it being red.

Azazel guffaws, glancing at the Judge. "You think I wasn't prepared for this? Join us! I've been expecting you." He spreads his arms out. Azazel's minions leap into the air, their fiery eyes burning as they descend upon the harrowing skulls of death.

I crouch and run toward Ambrose. I place my hands on his chest. "What do I do?"

He shakes his head. I try focusing on my magick. Despite being cuffed, there has to be something I can do to set him free. If my dagger can make sigils disappear, surely it can release Ambrose from Azazel's grasp? Azazel's distracted by the battle that has broken out, so this is my chance. I flip the dagger and squint my eyes in concentration. *Release him.*

Nothing happens.

I look at him and shrug. Amid the battle, I try to spot Dax, but there are too many of them in the way. I peek back down at the dagger when a strong surge of heat flashes through the room. My eyes shoot up and I spot my brother, standing in the middle of a pile of demon corpses. His eyes, pure fire, like something inside him ignited. He turns to face more of Azazel's minions rising from the ground and coming out of the walls. Since when did Dax have powers?

Sweat forms under my arms and my heart skips a beat. I turn back and focus again. "Maybe it's because there aren't any sigils on to focus on this time. With the door, I knew what to focus on, but now, I don't think I can single out the magick Azazel used to undo it." Ambrose coughs. Maybe I can at least give him his voice back.

Let him speak.

Ambrose pants hard, coughing and winded. A smile spreads across my face. "It worked!" I whisper, and quickly look back, making sure Azazel can't hear me. The fight is out of control. Reapers lay on the floor decapitated; demons are disemboweled and impaled on the walls. I search for my brother and Deacon but can't see either. The Judge is still pinned against the wall, watching everything, as Azazel intended.

"Addison," Ambrose finally whispers, stretching his jaw. I lean in and kiss him. For a few seconds, I tune out the screams and the clashing of weapons. For a moment, I pretend that everything is as it once was. That we're back at my place in the Keys, trying to teach him the references behind a joke we just watched in a movie. I pull away from his lips with tears in my eyes.

"I love you," he says.

"I love you too."

My desire for him becoming stronger seems to have set

the dagger off. It warms in my hand; I look down and to the hilt, glowing as it had done the night I conjured Paimon. I look back up and Ambrose is slowly being lowered on the ground. My will must have broken Azazel's spell. He wrapped his arms around me, squeezing me tight. Then he pulls away and looks out to the battle waging around us.

"We need to release the Judge," he says.

I nod and search for a clear opening. The loud banging of the iron doors makes my head turn. I stare back at the last Enochian sigil, barely managing to keep the doors shut.

"Addison, you can't open those doors."

"This might be the only way to end all this."

"No, you don't understand. Pure evil has been locked away in there for a millennium. Letting it out, uniting the planes, it'll be hell on Earth. Literally."

"No, that was Azazel's plan. But I'm the one with the dagger, and he said he can't do this without me. I can use it to put an end to this, once and for all."

Ambrose holds his breath. "I fear it won't be that easy. Go release the Judge. He might be able to help."

"What are you going to do?"

"I'm going to find your brother."

"No! It's too dangerous Ambrose!"

"There's no other choice." He pulls me in to kiss me one last time before letting go to join the battle.

I take a step back and nod before dashing toward the Judge. A demon intercepts me, and I slash at it with my dagger. It cuts right through it, orange light seeping out of its chest.

The Judge's sullen eyes peer deep into mine. I hold onto my dagger and concentrate on giving him back his voice.

"Even though I disapprove of your relationship, I do appreciate you, Addison."

My stomach clenches. "I don't know how to bring you down from the wall."

"It seems Azazel has dominion over all weapons and defenses in LLAPS. Allow me." He mutters a few words in a language I have never heard and lowers himself to the ground. Deacon rushes into view and tosses a scythe into the air. As the Judge grabs the scythe, the blade begins to glow blue. He inches the tip of the blade onto my wrists. "Don't move." I do as I'm told, and in two motions, the cuffs fall to the floor. I rub my wrists with my hands and look up at the Judge.

"Now, get out of here," he says. "We'll take care of this. Take Ambrose with you."

Can't argue with that. I want nothing more than to get out of dodge with my now human boyfriend. I turn to do just that and stop in my tracks at Azazel, staring at me. He flings a reaper he was holding by their throat in one hand.

My eyes widen with horror as Azazel conjures a spear and throws it directly at Ambrose.

"Nooo!" I dash out in the middle of the battleground. Dax reaches for me from behind and holds me back as Ambrose falls. I fight myself free from my brother's grip and run to Ambrose. I drop to the ground and lift his head off the stone floor and rest it on my lap. Blood gushes from the top of his chest, and he foams at the mouth as he tries to speak. I cover his wound, pressing down, trying to stop the blood. Dax places his hand on my shoulder.

"Addison, we have to go."

"No!" I yell.

"He wouldn't want you to stay here and get killed."

"I'm not leaving him here like this!" I say, tears streaming from my eyes.

"Deacon will take care of him, Addison. Listen to me, we have to go *now*!"

I lower my face to his, a tear dropping on his cheek. His crystal blue eyes gloss over as they peer into me. I lean in and kiss him until I can no longer feel his breath against my skin. I open my mouth and sobs pour out of me as I tremble uncontrollably. I hold on tight as my brother pulls me away from him.

TAKE THE REINS

ADDISON

The sound of clashing metal reverberates through my skull, causing my temples to throb in pain. I feel like my guts have been ripped out of me. My life, fallen apart again. My head is hidden beneath Dax's cloak as he shields me from the fighting around us.

"Addison, you're going to have to open a portal with your dagger," Dax says, bringing me back from my daze. Right, to go home . . . without Ambrose.

My palms grow damp. I fixate on the dagger, still covered in my boyfriend's blood. Dax leads me to the side of a wall. I don't look back to see if Azazel is after us. From the sound of my brother's voice, it's now or never. With a deep breath, trying to erase visions of Ambrose from my mind, I aim it at the wall.

A sliver of movement from an orange reflection catches my eye at the far end of the room. The last Enochian sigil waiting to be dismantled by my power. I look down at my dagger and then back at my brother.

"I'm sorry, but no. I'm not leaving."

His face stiffens. "What are you talking about?"

"I can still fix this."

"Addison, we have to hurry. What are you doing?" He grabs my shoulder as if trying to shake some sense into me. I move away from his grasp, turn toward the iron doors, and run for it. I sprint past the battle, ignoring the clashing and fighting. My brother yells out my name, but I ignore him. I don't care if I'm releasing the devil. Whatever evil he has planned behind those doors will be no match for the fury basking inside me.

My only priority right now is for Ambrose to live. I don't care about anything else. As a human or a reaper, as long as he comes back. What was it Azazel had said about light and dark? That I need both to open the door. I don't know if this is what he meant or if this will be enough, but it's what I've got.

As I approach the grand double doors, I remember everything good about Ambrose, taking in all the happy memories I felt with him. Then I shift my focus and allow my anguish and pain to fuel my drive and flood through my veins, into my dagger. The sigil burns bright as I focus all my attention on it. Did it work?

The sigil lets off a soft glow. And then it vanishes. A smirk appears on my lips and I lower my weapon. The fighting behind me stops. An uncomfortable silence falls, but I refuse to look back. My eyes burn through the doors as I reach for the handles.

The lock unlatches and I halt.

"Addison . . . step away from there," the Judge calls out. I stumble backward as the doors burst open.

Hot winds gush in from the other side, and I'm thrown backward onto the ground. Hungry flames burst out into the open and my vision blurs while I struggle to lift myself up to reach for the dagger. Its ruby hilt now glows bright red as I hold it close. I grab for my crane bag to hide it away, but it isn't there. My heart stops. It must have fallen out somewhere between my brief encounters with revitalizers and being trapped in the vines. Shit. How the hell am I going to take the dagger back now?

Alright, get it together. No time to panic. I grip the hilt of the dagger.

I watch as a tall, muscular man appears through the smoke.

His black hair is pulled back from his chiselled face. Long horns protrude from the top of his head, curved, facing backward, just like Azazel's. He steps in front of me and spreads out a pair of large, black, feathered wings. Leaning back on my elbows, I gaze at him, unable to move. He's magnificent.

Behind me, Azazel's minions gather around, bowing down before him. I watch as Azazel walks between them and approaches the winged devil.

"I knew you'd come around at the end, father." Azazel holds out his hand and a purple orb of light flashes in his palm. "I've now finished all the tasks you gave me. LLAP's prison has opened."

My lips part to speak but all I can muster is a stutter. Oh fuck, what did I do? Did I just help them open the portal to let demon's into Earth when he unites the planes? Azazel said the dagger would only open his father's cage. He lied about that too . . . Of course he did. How could I be so stupid?

"Not stupid. You released the power within you."

I gasp at the familiar voice. "That voice inside my head . . . That was you?" *I'm ready to get out of here with my brother and with Ambrose, alive.* I don't know if he can hear me, but he had before.

A smile spreads across his handsome face. "You're not finished yet."

"W–what do you mean?" I swallow. The literal devil is standing right in front of me. And *talking* to me.

"Don't you want revenge on the demon who killed your beloved Ambrose?"

"Revenge?" On his son? My eyes narrow.

Azazel quirks a brow at his father and they lock eyes for a moment, his face smug and unafraid. Okay, something's up.

Azazel turns to me, widening his stance. "That's right, Addie. Be angry with me. Give me your best shot." He puffs his chest out. "Come into your power," he urges. "Embrace your inner demon." I curl my lips. I can't even stand to look at him.

"He deceived you from the beginning, Addison." A condescending smile spreads on Lucifer's face. "Pretended to be your *friend* . . . pretended to *care* about you. Doesn't that boil your blood?" My eyes darken. Yes. Yes, it does.

My hands tighten around the now burning hilt of my dagger. Azazel sneers and I pause. Wait- he *wants* me to attack him . . . That doesn't make any sense. My eyes dart from him to Lucifer. Why do I get the feeling if I give into this I'll fall into their trap? "I thought I already embraced my darkness to release you," I say to Lucifer . . . What more do they want from me?

Dax finally speaks out. "He's manipulating you, Addison."

"Ah yes, Addison. Perhaps my helping you see clearly comes across as manipulation. But tell me, how do you think this will end?"

From the corner of my eye, a reaper closes in on them. Who is that? Dax? Deacon? My heart flutters.

Lucifer looks over his shoulder and waves his wrist. It's the Judge. With his scythe ready and attempting to reinstall all the Enochian enchantments.

A black mass manifests throughout the Judge's bones. It seeps over him, like a shadow, becoming solid as it spreads. Lucifer holds him afloat in front of everyone. The shadow grows thicker. Until it fully solidifies. The Judge's mandible drops off and hits the ground, turning to dust. One by one, the Judge's bones clatter on the ground, dissolving into dust.

"That was long overdue. Now, where were we?" Lucifer turns back to me, avoiding his son's gaze. I shoot a glance at Azazel when I catch him inching toward me.

Azazel struts over and looms atop the dusted remains of what once was the Judge. His eyes are dark. Distant. And without saying a word, he bends down and grabs for the golden scythe, glistening through the gray ashes.

My heart drums between my ears and I can hardly hear myself think. Is he about to become the new Judge? N–no . . .

A bright purple light emerges from the scythe. Azazel quirks a brow and his hand starts to shake. Veins ripple down his face from his horns, and down to his neck. He raises his eyes from the scythe and meets mine.

"H–help . . . "

Help? Me? Help *him*? I press my lips together and raise my chin. "I'd rather see you dead." The world turns red for an instant and I ball my fist at my sides, then step a few inches closer to him.

"No . . . wait!" Azazel cries. "I know where your father is!" The light seeps brighter out of his broken skin until it sweeps the room like dry grass catching fire. I shield my face as I land heavy on my back and skid across the floor to meet a wall. My breath hitches as Azazel cries out in pain. A sound I never heard a man make before and it scares the crap out of me. The light disappears and I lower my arms from my face.

"Son?" Lucifer grabs at his head and kicks the pile of dirt where Azazel had been standing. I wouldn't be able to make out if the ashes all belonged to the Judge or if Azazel's had now joined his. The scythe lays on the ground and a confused look of disdain falls on Lucifer's face.

I pick myself up and shoot a glance to where Dax is. I quirk a brow that hopefully reads to him as, 'What the hell just happened?' He locks eyes with me and shakes his head.

Somewhere among the horde of demons and reapers is Deacon with Ambrose's body. I step a foot in that direction and Lucifer holds a finger out. And suddenly, I'm glued to the floor. Oh God damnit.

He pinches the bridge of his nose, inhales, and then raises his chin.

I clear my throat. "W—what happened to Azazel?"

"That's my business for now." His face is rigid, his eyes narrow. I wish I could read his mind. He isn't acting like his son just died . . . Something has happened, but he isn't dead . . . is he? Not that I'd be complaining or anything.

My blood grows cold as I stare back at Lucifer. What are his plans with me? Is he going to kill me now since I didn't help his son when he asked? I gulp. Wrinkles crease my forehead as Azazel's last words permeate my thoughts. *I know where your father is* . . . I left my father at home. What does he mean?

A grin spreads on Lucifer's face and I shudder. Seriously? What's so funny? At a wave of his hand my feet loosen up and I can move again.

"Now, we're talking."

"What? I don't understand . . . What do you want with me?"

"Addison! Your eyes!" Dax yells. "They're . . . .red . . ."

"My eye—" I'm blinded by another vision of red

before my stomach lurches as I'm lifted off the ground. Maybe there was something more to my anger. Manic laughter permeates my skull as pain engulfs my entire body. My back bursts open, then the pains at my temples come next. I scream, but no words come out. Then, all at once, it stops. The pain subsides and energy surges through my body. Two strong arms bring me down from the air and lower me onto the ground.

As my vision comes back, stunned faces come into view. I jerk back as I realize that Lucifer is the one touching me.

A weight presses on my back. I twist my head and gasp. Large black and red wings stretch from my back.

"What the hell is this? What did you do to me?"

"You did this, Addison. I merely helped you complete yourself. And you are beautiful. Feel your strength and your now healthy heart! You will make a fabulous ruler."

Sweat rolls down my forehead as I clench my jaw. I move my hand toward my head to wipe it away and find my fingers wrapping around two curved horns on my head. I scream. What the fuck am I going to do? I can't go back home like this.

"Cheer up, Queen. You have been given a gift. Power."

Out in the distance, I spot Deacon hovering over Ambrose with her scythe in hand. Deacon shoots me a discerning look and brings her finger to her mouth, motioning for me to be silent. A portal opens behind them and she escapes with Ambrose in her arms.

I return my gaze to the devil.

"Don't worry, you'll get used to it." Lucifer raises his arms. Suddenly, the dark walls fall away, and we're surrounded by fields and fields of gray grass. Demons, minions, and guardsmen of all kinds stand in rows as far as my eyes can see. Lucifer stands tall before me and spreads his arms out.

"All ye unfaithful and unholy, bow down to your new queen and enjoy the gift of freedom. For now, all can leave and live on Earth if you so desire."

Dax runs over to my side and clasps my hand in his. I wince at him apologetically, unable to speak.

I peer up at Lucifer with wide eyes. "What if I don't allow them to leave? What if I use my power to keep them here?"

Lucifer grins. "You can't. You broke all the seals yourself. Besides, don't think you have all the power here. I said you are queen, as it's in your blood and you have the right. But I am still king, and now I am free." Lucifer spreads his wings, reaches up, flies to the purple sky and disappears through a portal.

My brother and I stand next to each other, watching as hordes of screeching demons take to the sky.

A gust of wind blows past us, followed by a ratcheting sound of a tornado. My hair blows around my face and my wings drop around me to protect my eyes. Peeking through the feathers, I see a swirling gray tower of clouds climb toward a gigantic portal in the sky.

"Addison, I don't think that's a normal tornado. They're the spirits from the prison."

All the tormented souls are rising, being released back onto Earth.

Dax turns and faces me. "What do we do now?"

"The only thing we can do. Take the reins of hell."

*H*owling winds blow against my face as we stand on a hilltop amidst the tremulous rise of what LLAPS has kept chained up and hidden since the beginning of time. I glance at my brother between my hair smacking against my face.

"We have to close it!" he shouts.

"How? I lost my dagger." My new wings weigh me down at my side. Closing it would mean being stuck down here . . . Without my dagger, I don't even know how to reopen a portal, let alone close this one. I move my right shoulder back, trying to keep my new wings from touching the skin on my face. They so readily like to wrap themselves around me, almost as if they have a mind of their own. How the hell am I even to go back like this? Will I forever have to stick to *Addison is going to wear a Halloween costume year-round? I* gaze up at my brother, who stares back at me with sorrowful eyes. So much has happened, I'm at a loss of what to do. Ambrose is gone, and I don't even know where Deacon has taken his body. *What was to happen with his body?* My breath seeps from my lungs as I watch

Ambrose die in my arms all over again. I had taken him being a reaper for granted. His words from the last battle with Ozo resonate in my mind: "The only thing that can kill me is the Judge's scythe or dragon fire." I was so sure I'd have him forever. That I would be his forever, or at least until I croaked. Nothing would be able to kill him. Until Azazel turned him human. I hate him. And I hate that I stabbed him, because it turned me into this demon thing.

A rumble of deep growls fights their way through the crowd of demons trying to get out. My attention snaps back to the present as hellhounds with pointed ears fly in, surrounding us. Enormous by nature, some of them reach Dax's shoulder standing up. These bitches are huge. With thick black fur, red eyes, and two rows of jagged teeth, they know they were made for destruction.

Dax's arms and eyes light up in flames as he powers up. "Aren't these the minions or hellhounds belonging to Azazel?"

"Think Azazel used some of them, but they just belong to the demons."

Dax holds out his arms and the hellhounds growl. Saliva droops down from their rows of sharp teeth as they near the hill on which we stand. Their pupils dilate with hunger, and I can see my own reflection in their eyes. More captives, demons, and creatures leave through the portal on the mauve sky.

"We're running out of time. What do we do?" Dax says as one hellhound jumps toward him.

"I think you're taunting them with all your fire. Calm down a bit."

"They must still be following Azazel's orders."

Another one leaps at him. This time, it clenches down on Dax's arm. Dax swings his arm back with full force. The pup lands with a thud but the others keep coming.

Now, a few jump at a time, too many for him to handle on his own. A rush of anticipation and rage surges through my bones. My wings spread out involuntarily, smacking my brother in the face. I can feel my eyes warming, I wonder if they're turning red. My chest heaves.

To my surprise, the hellhounds back down, circling around with their ears pointing down, as if cowering.

I jerk myself forward to threaten them, my attempts at scaring them off as if they were some bullies who just tried to steal my school lunch. Some ran off, while others stayed with their enormous heads hanging low.

"Get out of here!" I scream.

Some of the hounds kick dirt, tailing off, some cower but stay close by, ears hanging low, waiting to see if I meant it.

"Addie? How did you do that?" The fire in Dax's eyes dim until they go out completely, returning back to their normal brown color. I squint at one of the smaller of the few hounds that had just flown in from the distance when the hounds start to gather. Still large in size, but not as big as some of the rest, its head reaches my waist. Must be a puppy. It looks at me with droopy eyes while wagging its tail that can make the Earth shake. Despite its fierce red irises staring at me inquisitively, oozing with intelligence, I can sense a sort of sentience from it.

"Remember when Lucifer said these things now bow to me?"

"You mean you can control them?"

"I think so. Maybe control is a harsh word, but command them."

"Go on, tell it to do something."

I squat down and stick my hand out, beckoning for it to come forward. "Come here . . ."

The hellhound wags its tail furiously and runs over to

me. I recoil my hand, recalling what these dog-like creatures eat from my first encounter with them when I astral projected. The hound whimpers. It's hard to tell if it truly is sentient with its red eyes beaming back at me and shark-like teeth showing. I slowly move my hand out again. The beast slowly inches toward me, nudging his head under my hand. Gently, I begin to pet it behind his ears. I look up at Dax, whose face drops. "Guess this answers that question."

I continue to pet the hellhound while the mob of torment howls louder. More are coming. My brother lights up his hand only this time. It's getting worse. Something in the near distance catches my attention and I crane my neck to look. Among the hoard of imprisoned souls, demons, and burnt ones, something is gliding down.

"Addison, look over there. Another demon?"

I stand up and squint my eyes. "A bat? No, wait. That looks like Crowley!"

"No way!"

"Crowley!" we both shout, waving our arms.

I can't believe it. "Is it really him?" I ask.

"Yeah, it has to be. What are the chances of another Eastern screech owl flying around in LLAPS?" Dax swings his arms furiously. "Crowley!"

"What is he doing down here? I don't think he can hear us." My heart sinks. My father must have sent him after me. How long have I been in LLAPS? I join him in trying to call our familiar over. Crowley swoops down into the rubble, disappearing from view.

"Where did he go?"

"I don't know, but he'll know the way back."

"Addison, can you fly up there?"

I screw up my face and raise a brow, shooting him an angry look. "Are you kidding? I don't even know how to not hit you in the face with these things." I twist and turn, punching my new wings with both hands.

"Just thinking, maybe you can fly us up through the portal everyone is going through?"

I eye it. "Too dangerous. We'd get trampled and we don't even know where on Earth it leads to."

Dax passes a hand through his hair. "I'll be up there without my scythe too." He turns and scans the field. "Where are all the reapers?"

A pain stings my chest at the mention of the word *reaper*.

"I don't know, but if you had a scythe, this portal wouldn't be a problem. We could really use one or two right about now."

Dax nods in agreement. "I wish I had stashed one after the fight. There was no time though. Should we go back to the reaper quarters and see what I can find?"

"I don't even know how to get there, Dax. Do you? Lucifer just changed the scene and we were here. What if we're still in the same place, just a different dimension of it? This place is weird."

"Well, Addison. You're the one with the power now. You're our only hope."

I sigh and the hellpup howls. I touch my necklace like I used to when I wanted to call on Ambrose. A warm breeze passes through my hair, carrying the screams of tormented souls, and I clench my jaw. I need to think of something, a way to close that portal without the dagger, or without a scythe.

"I wish it would just close!" My wings burst open once more and Dax gasps. Silence strikes the arena and up above the portal has closed. Hundreds of creatures trying to escape now fall down to the gray field, some flying off, others landing with a thud.

The hellpup whimpers.

"Well, it's a start." Dax says.

I snap my mouth shut. "How the hell did I do that?"

"We'll wonder about that later. For now, can you open one just for us?"

I hold out my hand and say, "Portal, open."

Right in front of us, a portal swirls open, spinning clockwise until it's just an endless void of black.

"Perfect," says Dax, nudging my arm. "Come on."

The familiar smell of leather-bound books in our father's library welcomes us as we step back into Paradise House.

"It feels like ages since I've been back. How long do you think we were gone for?" I arch my head toward Dax, who's walking just behind me. His eyes grow wide as he enters through the hidden door of the library, making me spin around.

Our father is lying down on the couch, pale and cold to the touch.

"What has he done?" I run next to him, dropping my cloak on the floor and scraping the corner of the coffee table with my knee.

Dax places a hand on our father's head. "He's alive, but his spirit is gone."

"Is he comatose?" I press my ear against his chest.

"It seems so. He must have gone through the portal after you, Addie."

Tears well up in my eyes and I have a hard time biting

them down. *He's dying because of me.* "How long can he stay like this?" My voice cracks as I ask.

"That depends on how long he's been out of his body. He needs to get back soon."

"Why isn't he back yet? What if something happened to him?" I say, my voice breaking.

Dax falls silent. He walks over to the intercom and meddles with some of the buttons. I stay focusing on our dad.

"Now it makes sense why Crowley was there."

"Mhmm." Dax continues inspecting the library.

"He must have followed dad to make sure he was safe when he astral projected. Oh, why couldn't he just wait for me?" I say.

Dax is still quiet.

"Are you even listening?"

Dax, who is now crouching on the floor, looking under the couch, raises an eyebrow. "Does it feel hot to you?"

All the excitement had made me forget how cold the house usually is. I pick my hair up in a ponytail and feel the sweat drizzle down the nape of my neck. "Now that you mention it, yeah, it is pretty stuffy. What were you checking for?"

"Just hang on, wait here with dad." Dax opens up the library doors and disappears into the house.

Bringing my attention back to my father, I hold his hand tightly and study the purple veins on his eyelids. "I really wish you would have just stayed. Now how do I find you?" I climb to my feet and sit on the other couch acute to the one my father is on.

Time works differently in the astral plane. My stomach sinks at the thought of him being gone for hours. *I thought he said he didn't leave his body anymore.* My throat chokes with guilt, as I know it will be my fault if something happens to him. I had left a note in my room, just left. I grip onto my necklace, tracing the lines of the flower with my fingertips. My eyes grow heavy as I look toward the window, half expecting to see a purple sky. Within a few moments, I'm asleep.

Vivid images of weapons clashing in front of me hang in my mind. Azazel's horns protruding in front of my face. I fall to the floor screaming as I witness it all over again. Azazel stabbing Ambrose from behind. Ambrose, who had been human, who had lost his reaper power and went through hell to get back to me, his blood gushing over my hands and arms, out through his mouth. Then my wings burst out from my back.

I shudder and wake in a cold sweat, peering down at my arms where I had just been holding my boyfriend in my nightmare. I yawn and sit up, rubbing my eyes. I glimpse at my dad's sleeping body, taking shallow breaths. "Wherever you are, I hope you're okay," I whisper. My eyes widen as my arms begin to vibrate just a little.

A tingling sensation crawls up my spine and a slight cracking breaks the silence, causing me to snap my gaze to face a mirror on the bookshelf straight ahead. I squint and walk over, frost appearing to be cracking the glass. I touch it with my fingers and pull it back. The glass is frozen solid. The tingling sensation ceases. *This must have just happened now. Strange.*

Remembering my wings in my dream, I reach behind me, but there's nothing there. I turn myself around, trying to see myself in the half-frozen mirror. Nothing. Huh. Looks like they went away when I came through the portal. Relief sweeps over me. I knew I felt lighter.

I spin around and dash toward the sliding mahogany double doors. I begin pushing at one of the doors when Dax pops up out of nowhere.

"Shit, Dax. You scared me."

"Sorry, I was just coming back. What happened?"

"Check it out!" I turn around and lift the back of my shirt. "What do you see?"

"No wings," he says.

I turn back around and wrinkle my forehead.

"They probably appear best in the astral. But that's not to say you can't make them appear here. So be careful, Addison."

I clench my jaw. I know he's right. That would be a neat trick at parties, eh? "Right, okay. So, what did you find?"

"Well, there's no electricity in the neighborhood. Not sure if that's due to a storm that could have happened here or from . . ." He motions toward the secret door.

The chances of there having been a hurricane while I was gone wouldn't be the wildest thing to happen in Florida, but also, it isn't hurricane season. And a portal just released a shit ton of damned souls onto Earth . . . So yeah . . . there's that. "What do we do?"

"Well, for now, how long has it been since you slept? Or got some rest? You're still alive Addison, demon queen or not," he chides. "You need your rest or you're going to drop."

I shudder and pinch the bridge between my eyes, stifling a sneer. *Queen.* Not funny, Dax. The last thing on my agenda for my life is living and ruling LLAPS. "No, I'm fine. I just took a little nap. We have to go back to find dad, or his spirit rather."

"Nap? What was that, like the 20 minutes during the time I stepped out? There's no way you're going back now, with the state everything is in. I'll go back for him. You stay here and rest."

"Really, I feel fine. I've never felt more powerful in my

li—" A shuffling sound comes from within the library. Dax and I exchange a look and turn toward the sound.

"Did you hear that?" I ask.

"Shh." Dax silently walks back into the library. The scratching continues. I tiptoe behind him. "Dax, it's coming from the secret door."

We both moved in closer.

Shit, what could be out there trying to get in? Dax lifts a finger up to his lips as he inches toward the door.

"Ready?" I whisper. He gives me a nod.

I hit the button on the podium and Dax slowly pushes the door open. The dark void that leads to the astral plane lets out a swift breeze, a reminder of everything we had just endured.

A soft whimper comes from inside. My eyes move down toward the floor. A hellhound walks right inside, with its giant tongue hanging out its mouth, glowing red eyes popping out from the darkness. My jaw drops.

"Oh hell no. Get out of here!" Dax shouts. The hound sprints past him and into the house, its tail whipping furiously, knocking down figurines as it runs. Dax chases after it. "He'll destroy everything!"

I turn back to the open passageway and poke my head through to try and see if anything else had followed us in. The coast is clear. I push the door shut and lock it.

"Addison, what are you doing? Open it. We have to get this thing out."

The hellhound flies to the top of the chandelier, growling down at Dax.

"If I had my scythe, you'd be such a goner!"

Drool drops down from its large, pointed teeth and lands right on Dax's face.

I stifle a smirk at his appalled look. He wipes his face with his sleeve. "You're dead." Dax reaches up and grabs the bottom of the iron chandelier. The hellhound reaches out its giant paws and flies over his head and into the kitchen.

Pots and pans clash on the tile floor, falling from the overhead stove hooks. I slowly walk into the kitchen with both arms crossed, half expecting Dax to be wrestling with the beast from hell. I point an index finger at the hellhound. "You, stop!"

Both Dax and the beast stop to stare at me. The hellhound lowers its head and starts wagging its tail furiously again.

"Get off the stove," I say firmly.

The hellhound jumps down and crawls over to my feet. Dax's jaw hangs open.

"Why didn't you do that before?"

"Dax, this means a whole other issue."

He straightens his shirt, keeping his eye on the hellhound.

"The last time one of these things was in here, it tried to eat me."

"I know. That's why I was trying to kill it."

"Dax, you're not listening. That happened in the astral plane. When have you ever seen a hellhound able to walk into the physical plane like this?"

Dax raises an eyebrow. "When the portal was open, a lot of beings from there crossed through. This one followed us here."

"Exactly, so who knows what else is lurking around with its full abilities?"

The hellhound whimpers and extends its enormous tongue to lick my hand. I pull my hand back, wiping it on my clothes. "Stop it, I don't like slobber." The hound gives another whimper and drops its body on the floor. "I mean, this isn't just a dog. It's an enormous hound that can not only leap really high but can actually fly! We can't let this thing out."

"This is the same hellhound from out there . . . the one that came up to you."

"Yeah, I see that now, it's the same size. We'll lead it back to LLAPS when we go look for dad's spirit." I raise my fingers to my mouth to bite them, something my mother used to always do when she was under a lot of stress. I had wanted so badly to be back home, for all of this to be over, and now we had to rush back in to save our father. I spot Dax squinting at me and quickly bring my hand down. "Right, should we get going then?"

We turn to leave the kitchen when a high-pitched scream comes from outside.

I shut my eyes and sigh. "What was that?" I mutter under my breath.

We jolt down the stairs, the hellhound jumping over us and beating us to the door.

"No, stop it, stay back." Its whipping tail rips lacerations on my legs. I move to shield myself from getting hit and grab onto the hound's head to try to pull it behind me while Dax slowly opens the front door and pokes his head out. I struggle to fight the hellhound back. Springing from its hind legs, it shoves me back and topples Dax over as it jolts through the door. We both watch in horror as the hound breaks through the green iron gates as easy as if it were breaking through thin glass.

I get up from my knees, shoving past my brother after the beast, but I'm way too slow. The hellhound is just joyously leaping through the air, catching wind and flying down the neighborhood.

"This is a catastrophe. What if someone sees it?" I run out to the street, forgetting about the initial scream I had heard. Dax shuts the door behind us.

The neighborhood is quiet. Not a car in sight. I stand in the middle of the street and move my eyes from window to window of the houses. Something's off. *What day is it? Maybe they are all at work and at school?*

"Where is everybody?" I ask Dax as he catches up to me on the road.

"Where did the giant pup go?"

I shake my head and shrug. "Does the neighborhood seem . . . quiet to you?"

"Yeah, it's giving me the vibe of the calm before a hurricane hits."

"Hmm . . . maybe there is an actual hurricane coming. I'm getting the same vibe."

"It would explain the loss of power." Dax chafes his chin.

Someone screams in the house next door.

"Wishful thinking, let's go!" I dash for the next-door neighbor's house and start banging on the door. I try the handle but, like a smart Floridian, the door is locked.

"Mrs. Willson? Mrs. Will—"

"Step aside." Dax moves me over with his hand and kicks the door in.

We walk in slowly at first. I check the downstairs. The living room is spotless, with straw furniture and a glass-top coffee table. All of the appliances are off in the kitchen, no indication that anyone has cooked a meal or used a dish.

"Addison, I'm going upstairs," he says.

"I'm right behind you."

The floorboards creak as we make our way up the wooden staircase. "Mrs. Willson?" I call. A growl comes from one of the rooms. Dax moves his index finger to his mouth, motioning for me to be quiet. He slowly twists the doorknob; the hinges give a low whistle as he pushes the door open.

Glass is shattered all over the opposite end of the wall and the window has been broken.

A hoarse voice resonates from the corner shadow of the bed. "Begone, beast!"

Mrs. Willson lays on her back, not moving. Her eyes, bloodshot red and wide open, her lips pale and dry as her mouth hangs open. I gasp and look over to what is hovering in the corner.

The dark mass floats closer to our neighbor, a long hood flowing behind it. It ignores us, looking at Mrs. Willson's body, moving its arms out toward her. "Don't just stand there," it hisses at us. "Collect your beast."

Shocked, I turn my head to the hellhound that's showing its teeth at the demon's robes.

"That's not my beast. Let Mrs. Wilson go. Now!"

Dax moves in closer to me, emphasizing I'm not alone.

"Not your beast?" The demon snickers.

"I'm warning you, leave her alone!" I take a step forward, and Dax holds out his hand to stop me.

The demon laughs. "It's too late. Her spirit is mine."

I run over to my neighbor and grab her hand as I watch Mrs Wilson's spirit lift above her body. I shake the old lady's hand, calling her name and trying to get her to wake up. Maybe if I could jolt the spirit back into her body . . .

"You're wasting your time. She's under my paralysis charm," it hisses.

"Why are you doing this?' Dax shouts.

The hellhound jumps into the air and slurps up Mrs. Wilson's spirit, swallowing it down in two gulps. My face pales.

"Nooo!" The demon moves back and screeches, the same screaming we heard outside the house. "You ruined it, with your stupid hound!"

"Again, not ours." I let go of my neighbor's cold hand. I'm shaking. Dax comes in and closes Mrs.'s Wilson's eyes on her face.

I'm panting. I switch my gaze over to the hellhound, who's licking its lips. It stops to look at me and begins wagging its tail.

"You . . . ate . . . my . . . neighbor!"

The hellhound starts to back up when I charge at it.

"Addison, no!" Dax yells. It's too late. The hound jumps back out the window. Damnit!

Dax turns to face the demon. "Who are you and what are you doing here?"

"I'm . . . Shebash and I'm a soul collector. Now, I have to find someone else."

I pinch the bridge of my nose and swallow a breath. "I thought I commanded you to stop. Why didn't you stop?"

Shebash laughs. "You don't command me. I was just following orders."

I arch a brow and glance at Dax.

"Didn't you hear Lucifer? You take orders from your new queen now." Dax says.

"I don't take orders from that angel, fallen or not. He'll never be one of us. And I . . .—" The demon hovers closer. "—certainly do not take orders from you," he spits.

I wince. There goes that idea.

"Who commands you then?" Dax demands.

Shebash zooms around to face Dax. "Where's your scythe, reaper?" The demon shows its teeth from the dark, hooded shadow of his cloak. He gives a hoarse laugh and then disappears, leaving us with our dead neighbor.

Son of a bitch. "What do we do now?"

Dax wipes his face, shrugs, and stares out the hole of the broken bedroom window. "We go find Little Feet, I guess."

"Little Feet?"

"I don't know. We'll need to call it something. Little Feet, because it's huge. It's ironic, don't you get it?"

"Yeah, I get it." I shake my head. "Even if we *were* keeping it, I wouldn't name her Little Feet."

"Her?"

"Yes, if you hadn't noticed, it is a she." I lower my eyes at Mrs. Wilson's body. "Poor lady, she didn't deserve this."

"No, she didn't. She was old and was soon to die, anyhow."

I shoot him an angry glance.

"But she did deserve a proper reaping." Dax says quickly. "So how do we get things back to normal?"

"I don't know, but one thing is for sure. We need to find Lucifer to get him to put everything back to the way it was." I gulp. "Especially me."

*Turn the page to read the
first chapter of Blood of Demons, the
third book in the series.*

LIFE AFTER DEATH

AMBROSE

Silence falls upon my cohorts as I stand front and center in the Reaper Council courtroom. Their hollow eyes glare back at me—the reaper who was turned human and killed by Azazel's hand. Everyone, including me, had expected me to be dead. But here I am, with my hood down, and in my human skin. But I am not human.

I shut my eyes, attempting to block out the chatter echoing through the room. Images of reapers and demons warring upon one another still flash across my memory. One minute, I was human, having gone through extreme temperatures in the Savannah desert, and then feeling the grief of losing my memory. The next, I was stabbed in the back and dying in my beloved girlfriend's arms, until she was pulled away by her brother to save her life. I squeeze my eyes tighter. *My poor Addison. Where are you?*

"Do you think this is some kind of evolution?" someone asks.

Someone else scoffs. "Evolution? This is an abomination. Reapers cannot fall in love with humans." The murmurs continue as I stand and wait patiently for Deacon to arrive.

A bony hand presses down gently on my shoulder. I open my eyes to Deacon's icy stare and then she gives me a nod. Her red bangs fall straight down to her cheeks. She's in human form as well. I nod back and follow her behind the podium where our late Judge's scythe lies flat.

Deacon grabs the gavel and bangs it on the table three times. The courtroom falls silent again.

"There is a reason why this council meets in a courtroom," Deacon begins. I take a few steps away from the podium, to let Deacon have her dramatic introduction. I'm tired of being the focus of attention. I stare at her with the rest of the reapers. She raises her hood over her head as her eyes sink back into their sockets, leaving only the hollow gaze of a skull. Her skin dissipates as her skeletal figure emerges.

"We make decisions for not only our council, and for humankind, but also for the entirety of LLAPS." She pauses and glimpses at the audience of reapers. Some are sitting with arms crossed, others tapping their feet anxiously.

"Last night we joined together in hand-to-hand combat against Azazel and his league. We did something that hadn't been done in a millennium since our late Judge sentenced Azazel himself to the cages."

"What about Lucifer?" someone calls out. Deacon holds out her hand.

"Lucifer will be found and dealt with."

"What do we do now without the Judge?" someone else says.

"Yeah, who is going to give the orders with him gone?" says another.

Deacon hits the gavel on the podium. "Please, I know

you have many questions, and I will try my best to answer them. As you all know, I have been the Judge's right-hand reaper for hundreds of years. I see it suiting that I take up his scythe and continue his work as Judge. Does anyone object?"

Silence spreads among them as they all look at one another.

I mean obviously, who else would it be? This is what he has been training her for. I lift my hands to clap.

"Hold on." A voice comes from the far end of the courtroom.

Deacon furrows a brow bone. "Yes? Uhh . . . Lorcan?"

I resist the urge to roll my eyes. Lorcan has always had opposing opinions when it suits him but pretends to be on par with all of reaper law. He's had it out for me since even before I went after Abyzou. Lorcan stands up from the end and points to me. Great, here it comes. "How did he come back to life? And is he still human?"

I scowl at Lorcan. All the other reapers stare me down. I shoot a look at Deacon and then back to the audience. I open my mouth, but Deacon cuts me off.

"Right. Under the hand of Azazel, Ambrose was turned human, only to be killed in battle after he had come back to aid us. But—I noticed he wasn't dead yet. But dying. I returned him to the Akashic waters where he was rejuvenated back to himself.

"Back to himself? So then, as reaper?"

"I'll answer that, Deacon." I take a few steps forward and peer through the audience until my eyes meet with Lorcan's. "Yes, Lorcan, I am back to being a reaper."

Lorcan curls his lips, locking his eyes with me as he speaks. "Well then, I suppose we have you to thank, Deacon, for saving one of our fellow . . . brothers." His gaze finally frees mine and turns to all the others. "I would not be opposed to following Deacon in our late Judge's place." Lorcan darts his eyes back to mine one more time before sitting back down, and I quirk an eyebrow in return.

"Any other questions?" Deacon asks.

Someone else stands up. "After it all happened, some of us still don't have our scythes."

"Ah yes, I have collected the scythes that Azazel had confiscated and will return them to all of you right after this meeting is adjourned."

The council claps.

"In that case," Deacon raises her voice, "with the power of myself and this council of Reapers I declare myself Judge of the Reaper Council." Deacon straightens her back and the council grows silent, in anticipation of Deacon grabbing the scythe.

I smile as I watch Deacon place her hand on the hilt, slowly taking in the moment. If there was ever a reaper who was a rule-following servant to the order, it was Deacon. She's going to make a fine Judge. I wonder who she'll have as her right hand.

A red, burning light washes over the courtroom. Deacon shouts as she's flung into the wall. Angry welts rise on her hand. Members of the council stand, jaws dropped. The Judge's golden scythe is about to hit the ground. I leap through the air to keep it from hitting the floor, not thinking about the possible repercussions.

The scythe lands perfectly in my hand. And as it hits, I wince, expecting it to sear my palm the way it did hers. Instead, it glows a bright, powerful blue that lights up my face. The energy from the scythe pulses through my body, lifting me up. My human skin sinks deep into my bones, revealing my hollowed eyes and sleek mandible. The courtroom gasps and watches in horror.

Deacon pushes up and steps forward, in awe. She clears her throat. "It looks as though the scythe has chosen its owner instead."

All eyes are on me as I come down to my feet. My eyes never leave the scythe and my lips part shock reverberating through my bones.

"This has to be a mistake," I sputter out. "I can't be the Judge."

Lorcan vaults to his feet, sending his chair clattering to the floor. "Absolutely not. I refuse to follow a reaper who fell in *love* with a human. He's broken every rule in the book! Do we not all agree?"

The courtroom erupts into protests.

"Agree or disagree!" Deacon bangs the gavel on the podium as she collects herself from having hit the wall. "Perhaps Ambrose's experiences have caused the Judge's scythe to choose him, or for reasons unknown. Be it as it may, you all saw what it did to me when I touched it."

A few of the reapers grumble, but Deacon ignores them. "I believe this leaves no choice. Ambrose has to be the Judge."

So much for not wanting to be the center of attention. "No, no I can't be the new Judge." Walking closer to the podium, I lean toward Deacon. "This has to be a mistake," I hiss, eyes darting over the leering crowd. "As Lorcan said, I–I've never exactly had respect for the laws, I don't even want to be in LLAPS. Deacon, we have to find a way for you to take it. Let's go to the Akashic waters. Just you and me—"

"Enough, Ambrose. Don't let anyone hear you," Deacon says, dropping her voice to a whisper. She sighs. "To be honest, it doesn't surprise me much that the scythe chose you."

My eyes widen.

"Think about it. You're a reaper who has lived a

human experience. You've seen both ends and rose from the dead, practically. It makes perfect sense."

"Deacon, I believe you will make a far better Judge than I."

"Well, that doesn't matter now, does it? As much as I was ready to take on that scythe," she says, pointing at it in my hands, "I am willing to let the rightful person bear it and follow them just as I did with the Judge. My purpose is to serve the council. I don't care much about power."

I lend her a scornful look. "Deacon, I need to leave and check on Addison. She thinks I died as a human!"

Deacon scoffs.

"You saw her! When I was dying, you got to see what happened, didn't you? Tell me, is she okay?"

"Enough! Ambrose, you need to put her behind you. Addison is fine. She's currently with her brother. Your new role holds a much greater responsibility. The entire council depends on you to return order to LLAPs. You need to pick yourself up and assume your rightful position as Judge." Deacon softens her eyes and sighs. "Look Ambrose, this might be your opportunity to change what you didn't agree with. Make a difference."

Deacon's words resonate with me. What am I to do? The scythe chose me to rule the council. She's right.

Deacon grabs me under my right arm. "Get up here and say something."

I stammer as Deacon steps down from the podium. Every reaper's eyes are fixed on me. I swallow as their icy, cold stares drill into my skull. After a moment, chatter fills the room, sending shivers down my spine. My knees quiver.

"Ahem," Deacon whispers at me.

I blink, shaking off my confusion and ignoring their ear worms. *OK, here goes.* I pick up the gavel, mimicking what

Deacon had so readily done before, and bang it on the podium three times. Their talking tapers off.

"Well, is he going to speak?" Lorcan asks.

"Yes, Lorcan. I will speak," I say, shooting him a sardonic glance. The smug reaper sits back, pursing his lips. "Thank you all for your patience. I–I find myself at a loss for what to say. This is all highly unexpected. To be honest," I stammer, "I would prefer it if Deacon were Judge, as she has the most experience, having been our dearest Judge's right hand for so long. Hell, I think Deacon here is the only one who knew his name. We all just called him Judge."

"It was Silas . . ." Deacon says.

A few of the reapers in the back offer a laugh.

"So, what are you going to do to put things right?" Lorcan stands up again. All eyes land back on me, some nodding in agreement.

I look at my new golden scythe. Deacon's words run through my mind again. *This might even be your opportunity to change what you didn't agree with. Make a difference.* I clear my throat.

"I'm going to change a few of the rules about the way we do things."

"Like what? Are you going to allow us to date humans?" Lorcan scoffs, followed with a laugh.

"Now that you mention it, Lorcan, I do intend to change that strict law. You will no longer be persecuted for fraternizing with humans or spending time on Earth. I'm not saying *date humans*. But getting to know humans better will do you all a bit of good. You can all stand to learn a little empathy." Reapers from all corners of the room gasp. Lorcan screws up his face.

"And as for the first order of business. After a quick recess, you will all retrieve your scythes from Deacon and will resume reaping past due deaths on Earth. Millions of people still suffered at the hands of Azazel, and we were not able to do our jobs when their time came. Those spirits need to be directed." My eyes dart around the room. Reapers nod in agreement. My spirits lift. "Azazel has caused enough pain as it is, and we're wasting time talking about it. Secondly, I will need two search teams. One will be for the sole purpose of finding any rogue spirit and bringing them back to LLAPS. The second team will hunt any demons who left the portal and annihilate them."

Deacon coughs and shoots me a look.

"Yes, Deacon?"

"Annihilate them, Ambrose?"

"Correct. Annihilated." I continue. "Next order of business will be to guard the Akashic waters and put guardsmen on alert for anytime a portal opens. We can't take any chances with what could have escaped LLAPS."

"All demons?" Lorcan stands up, a sly smile spreads across his face.

"Ambrose, if I may," Deacon interrupts, "the demons are just creatures from LLAPS . . ."

"Let me repeat myself. Nothing that came out of there was good, and the way to end it is to kill all of them. Any demon with the sense to stay behind will have."

Deacon falls silent and shoots Lorcan an angry look. I quirk a brow at her.

"Deacon, you hate the demons. Why are you so concerned about me killing them off?"

She shakes her head at the crowd, and I scrunch my brows.

"They're LLAP'S creatures, is all. I'd be careful with bending the rules so much. Keep in mind there is an order and a purpose for all things, malignant or not."

"They've caused more damage than good." I raise my

voice, turning to the council. "As I said before, I do intend on making changes."

Lorcan leans in on his seat. "Exterminating demons is something I can get behind."

A smile curls up my lips.

The good news? The rescue mission was successful. The bad news? Not only did Ambrose come back, so did all of the underworld.

Monsters roaming my neighborhood sure brings a new meaning to the phrase "Hell on Earth."

Apparently, my little "detour" awakened my demon blood. Now my magick is on the fritz AND I'm first in line to be the queen of demons. But growing horns isn't nearly as easy as accepting a crown.

Oh yeah, and my boyfriend? He wants my head on a platter.

Before I deal with him though, I've got to put Hell's creatures back where they belong. Or else everyone I love will pay the price.

The Judge thinks imprisonment can subdue the Angel of Death. He's an expert at underestimation.

Unfortunately, my ticket to freedom is a screeching, child-stealing demon. Do I dare lull her into submission, just to help my betrayer of a father? Even if it means exposing my deepest, darkest secret?

Desperate times call for desperate measures.

Available in all major eBook stores.

One phone call landed me the perfect job. Too bad it didn't come with life insurance.

I didn't think this job would be anything special. Sure, the first phone call was weird, and yeah, maybe it wasn't the smartest idea to come to someone's house before I met them in person, but Dax seemed nice. All he wanted was a caretaker for his sick father.

Oh, and an exorcist for the spirits haunting his family's estate. Now he's left me alone with his father, and the ghosts know my name. Caring for an old man with dementia, I can do. Fighting evil spirits? That's way above my pay grade.

But Dax has disappeared so I have to learn on my own or both Orlando and I might not live to see tomorrow . . .

Available everywhere they sell books.

Dear human,

I didn't see it coming. When Azazel pushed me through the portal, the last thing I thought was that I'd end up in the Jordan desert, completely stripped of my powers. I was human and I never felt so much pain and suffering.

Right now, I can't tell Addison what happened because Deacon whisked me away to try to save me… and during my last dying breaths, all I can think about is how much pain Addison is going through having watched me get stabbed. Would you like to read about what happened while I was in the desert? You're the only other human I can talk to who could relate….

Get the prequel free when you sign up for Killian's mailing list at http://killianwolf.com/

Falls on the floor

I cannot believe this book is finished. After writing it the first time under a separate title, and then unpublishing it and reworking the whole thing, I almost didn't think this day would come!

For my Urban Fantasy lovers, I know this book took you out of Earth, and believe me, Addison hates my guts. Not only for throwing her into another dimension and away from her Cuban coffee, but for putting her in the most awkward situations! I swear I could hear her cussing out my name while writing it. I hope you still enjoyed it all the same. Book three, *Blood of Demons*, will be back in the Florida Keys.

First, I'd like to thank my editor who has been a total dream to work with. The way this book transformed from what it was when it was the Scapegoat Demon to now is unbelievable. Claerie, I could not have done this without you. Thank you for taking the time to brainstorm with me, put up with me during my crazy moments of panic every time I found a plot hole, and for helping me create what is now this book that I can be proud of.

To my husband, thank you thank you thank you for being so patient while I continue dragging you through my author journey. We're in this together, and I promise it'll all be worth it. I love you to the Death Star and back—always.

To Ash the Silent, both your worldly and otherworldly wisdom speaks to me as a conscience on my shoulder. Your teachings of the runes, ogham, and Sabbatic philosophy have inspired me in many facets of this series and they will stay with me forever. Thank you for your love and support, and for always believing in me.

A huge thanks to all my friends and family who have shared my books with everyone—your support means the absolute world to me.

And finally, thank you to you, the readers who took a chance on my books and have read up to the second book in this series. I hope that by reworking the original, giving it a fresh coat of paint, that I can get it to more hands. Thank you for being a part of this and for sticking with me. I hope you're enjoying Addison's journey as much as I love writing it. If you get the chance, I would love it if you could leave a review where you bought it from.

Stay tuned for a sneak preview of the third book in the series, *Blood of Demons*.

THANK YOU

Thank you for reading *Lying With Demons*. I hope you enjoyed Addison's adventure as much as I loved writing it. If you did, I would be really grateful if you could spare a few minutes to leave a review on the site you bought it from. Reviews mean the world to authors.

If you would like to receive updates on all my new releases, please join my mailing list at http://killianwolf.com/. You will also get access to my books at a discounted launch price when they first come out, along with an exclusive sneak peek or short story just for you.

GET IN TOUCH!

Please feel free to get in touch with me.

Website: http://killianwolf.com/

facebook.com/killianwolfauthor

twitter.com/killian_wolf22

instagram.com/killian_wolf_author

pinterest.com/killianwolf22

goodreads.com/killianwolf

amazon.com/Killian-Wolf/e/B07WHFB8FW

bookbub.com/authors/killian-wolf

ABOUT THE AUTHOR

Killian Wolf is a Miami, Florida, native who enjoys pirates, rum, and skulls as much as she loves writing about dark magick and sorcerers. She holds a Bachelor of Arts degree in Cultural Anthropology and Sociology and a Master of Science in Environmental Archaeology and Palaeoeconomy.

Killian writes books about obtaining magickal powers and stepping into other dimensions. She lives in England with her husband, a tornado of a cat, and the most timid snake you'd ever meet. When she isn't writing, you might find her at an archaeological dig, rock climbing, or sipping on dark spiced rum while working on a painting.

GLOSSARY

Akashic level: The Akashic level is considered a neutral zone where demons are not meant to enter.

Akashic water: Eternal and universal knowledge is stored here.

astral plane (also known as the fifth dimension, astral world, astral dimension): Realm of existence where spirits go after they leave Earth. Also known as the "in between" or space between physical realms. It is divided into two halves, higher and lower levels.

astral projection: The ability to leave one's body and enter the astral plane in spirit form.

athame: A small dagger used for magick

and ritual purposes. In paganism, it acts as a wand, but possesses the element of fire rather than wind. It can act as a magickal tool to channel one's energy while carrying the magickal attributions of the dagger, including any sigils or stones it possesses.

curse*:* A negative form of spell intended to do a person or place harm.

demon (*demonio* in Spanish)*:* An entity born in the lower level of the astral plane which has tendencies for evil. Some feel they are often misunderstood.

egregore*:* A life-form created by the brewing of negative human emotions over a long period of time. They eventually become poltergeists if allowed to live for too long.

Enochian*:* Divine language spoken by dwellers of the astral planes.

Enochian sigil*:* Enochian scriptures bound together to form written spells, often used by demons or sorcerers.

Goetia*:* Grimoire on the practice of demonology.

Grimoire*:* Text that holds magickal spells and incantations, including but not limited to the creations of talismans, servitors, and the conjuring of entities.

lesser-lower-demon: Demon with little intelligence, akin to pets or thralls to higher-level demons.

LLAPS (Lower Levels of the Astral Planes): The bottom half of the astral dimension. The energy source of all negative forces, and the birthplace of demons.

Magick: Magic spelled with a "k" was first written in the early twentieth century by Aleister Crowley to differentiate the difference between "magick," as in to give energy direction, and "magic"'s as stage tricks.

portal: A forced breach into the astral dimension.

reaper: Operative dispatched to collect souls for the purpose of guiding them to their path. They are stationed in the Akashic level of LLAPS, near the higher astral levels.

sorcerer: Practitioner of magick, often known to conjure, create servitors, and open portals.

scythe: Tool used by the reapers to open

portals, collect souls, and connect with other reapers. Reaper lore suggests that the original scythe was once used in war and can channel energy in either direction. The golden scythe, the scythe used by the Judge, is the only scythe powerful enough to kill another reaper.

servitoire*:* Life-form created by the concentration of a human emotion for the purpose of serving a sorcerer/sorceress.

sigil*:* A symbol crafted by a magickal practitioner intended for a specific desired outcome. These symbols are often private to the practitioner, encompassing a particular scripture or blend of different scriptures, including ones that can be made up. It is often difficult to break a sigil if a different practitioner of magick cannot decipher the sigil, especially when it has been sealed with blood magick.

spell*:* Energy given direction, often but not always in the form of a spoken word.